THE GARAN
DIVINATION

C. A. Breheny

ISBN: 0692363599
ISBN 13: 9780692363591
Library of Congress Control Number: 2015900245
Breheny Publishing, North Haledon, NJ

To my mother, for being the best example of emotional strength.
To my father, for always being there for me.
To Megan and Diana, for believing in my imagination.
To my husband, for making me smile.
To my family, for supporting me.
To Gabby, Ally, Giuli, & Andrew, for keeping me young at heart.

1

Fall 1978

Erin pushed open the front door of her house and stepped into her living room. It was not a big house, but it was much more spacious than the New York City two-bedroom apartment her family had lived in several years prior. The first floor of the house was similar to a railroad-apartment layout, with a living room and kitchen divided by a bathroom on the left and a staircase on the right. From her first step inside, Erin saw her older brother and sister were already in the kitchen, scavenging for an afternoon snack. David and Lisa were in high school and got out of school earlier than Erin, so they always arrived home before she did. Her stomach growled as she put her book bag down by the door.

Erin knew that David and Lisa would push her out of their way if she tried to make a snack, so she ran up the stairs toward the bedroom she shared with Lisa to get changed into her playclothes. Erin saw her mother folding and putting away towels in the hall closet and greeted her with a quick hug.

"Remember to hang up your jumper so it doesn't get wrinkled," her mother said as she was closing her bedroom door.

"I will," Erin shouted as she quickly undressed. She carefully hung up her school uniform, a black-checkered jumper, and tossed her light-blue blouse into her laundry basket. Erin pulled on her hand-me-down jeans and put on her favorite white T-shirt with the yellow smiley face. She took a quick look in the bathroom mirror and pushed the brush through her hair. She hated her boy-short, feathered hair and wished she had the "Dorothy Hamill" haircut the other girls in school had. Erin decided she would beg her mom to let her hair grow out the next time she was due for a haircut, and she headed back downstairs to the kitchen.

The rest of the kids in their neighborhood went to public school and were home about an hour before Erin's Catholic elementary school let out. Erin saw the other kids playing a game of Kick the Can on her walk home from the bus stop and was hoping they would be playing by the time she got outside. She hurried to smear peanut butter on a few saltines and poured herself a glass of milk.

Erin ate way too fast and gulped the whole glass of milk as she stood up to put the glass in the sink. She was excited that she was seconds from playing with her friends, and when she heard her father's car pull into the driveway, her excitement turned to joy. She ran at full speed out the front door and down the walkway, and almost tackled her dad with a hug as soon as he stepped out of his car.

Erin's dad, Owen McGowan, hugged her tightly and asked, "Why aren't you playing with the other kids?" Owen had worked a double shift, yet his uniform was still neat, and he wore a huge smile on his face when he saw his daughter.

Erin smiled, looked lovingly into her dad's hazel eyes, and said, "I just finished my snack, and I am going over there right now!"

"Wait—say cheese," Erin's mom said.

Erin spun around and saw her mom on the front step of the house, waiting to take their photo with her new camera. Erin's dad put his arm around her shoulders, and they both smiled and said "cheese" as commanded. There was a momentary flash as the camera emitted a popping sound.

Satisfied, Erin's mom said to herself, "I hope I'm using this the right way." Then she walked back into the house.

Owen smiled at Erin and said, "You better hurry and get some playing in before dinner."

Erin started skipping toward the end of the street where the kids were playing and then turned and looked back at her dad. Erin paused as she watched her dad loosen his tie and unbutton the top of his shirt. The metal charm her dad wore on his neck revealed itself and shone as it reflected the afternoon rays of sun. She then remembered her question and yelled, "Can we get breakfast at Don's Deli tomorrow?"

Her dad smiled and gave her a nod before he turned and walked into the house. Erin thought about how much she loved her dad as she hurried over to her friends.

Erin's curiosity was endless, and over time she had tried to learn everything she could about her father. Owen was born the third of six children raised by poor Irish immigrants in New York City. He was born at a simpler and safer time, about a decade before the baby boomers.

Owen constantly told stories of the South Bronx neighborhood where he had lived and how he and his brothers used to be able to play in the streets, ride the train, and go anywhere they wanted to, unsupervised, even as young children. He said that things were different then. Everyone in their neighborhood knew one another, and the kids behaved because they knew any mischief would be reported back to their mothers.

Owen had started his career as a san man—sanitation worker or garbage man—as most entry-level sanitation workers do, picking up garbage cans and driving a garbage truck. He was gradually promoted to driving a sanitation-sweeper truck, then to foreman, and finally to superintendent in charge of managing the workers responsible for garbage collection on the west side of Manhattan.

Erin could not help noticing that her father cheerfully worked long hours and was proud of doing a good job. Erin saw him leave the house looking professionally dressed in his perfectly pressed uniform and loved that he always returned home with a smile, no matter how many hours he had worked. At ten years old, Erin viewed her father as the best man ever born and wanted to be just like him.

One of the most common questions adults ask children, and Erin heard it often, was, "What do you want to be when you grow up?"

Erin was always delighted with this question and answered by holding her head high and exclaiming, with as much pride as if she were saying she was going to be the president of the United States, "I am going to be a garbage woman!" It was only in the past few months that Erin had noticed the reaction that adults had to this response. She was still wondering why a few people had cringed when they heard this response. Did they not know how wonderful her father was?

Erin put this thought out of her head when she met up with the other neighborhood children just as they were chanting the count-down for the next session of Kick the Can. All the children chant-ed, "Five, four, three, two, one!" Then one of the bigger boys in the neighborhood kicked the plastic milk jug filled with pebbles, and everyone—except the younger girl who was "it"—ran to find a hiding spot in the surrounding area. Erin blocked all her thoughts and ran like she was on fire to her trusty hiding spot behind the neighbor's shed.

The game continued until Erin heard her mother's unique, loud whistle calling her home for dinner. Erin immediately turned and ran home.

As she walked in the front door, she heard her mother say, "Wash your hands." Erin lined up behind her brother and sister in the bath-room. She came to the table with clean hands and the smell of fall on her skin. She was happy after playing and was ready to eat. Her father sat at the head of the table, and her mother rushed about gathering items for the meal.

Owen jovially asked, "How was everyone's day?"

Lisa jumped at her chance to be the center of attention and quickly said, "I learned in school today that we are technically Irish Mafia!"

Erin had previously watched a few scenes from the movie *The Godfather* and was horrified to hear Lisa's announcement. Owen laughed when he saw Erin's expression, and Lisa looked at Erin and yelled, "Don't be such a baby, Erin! The Irish Mafia is not a real Mafia!"

Lisa continued in her know-it-all voice, "The term 'Irish Mafia' was used to describe how the civil service jobs in New York City were basically all taken by Irish Americans. That's why we are Irish Mafia on Dad's side of the family. Think about it: Uncle Kevin is a New York City police officer, Uncle Sean is an New York City fireman, and Dad is an New York City sanitation worker."

Erin digested the information but couldn't help being annoyed with Lisa for thinking she knew everything.

Owen quickly changed the subject and asked, "Erin, how is your tooth? Does it hurt?"

Erin had forgotten about the toothache she had experienced a few days prior and said, "It's OK. It hasn't hurt since the other day."

Owen continued, "Well, I think you should still get it checked out tomorrow. I know you have never had a cavity, but it's better to be safe than sorry."

Lisa quickly joined in. "I don't think it's fair that Erin gets to miss school tomorrow!"

Lisa was rarely jealous of anything Erin had, and Erin couldn't help feeling pleased with being able to take a day off from school and spend it with her dad. Although Erin lived in New Jersey, the dentists covered by her father's health insurance were only in New York City. Thus, a typical trip to the dentist would include going with her father to work on a day off from school.

Owen continued, "If Erin's toothache is from a cavity, it's better to fix it early. Erin will have to catch up on the work she misses at school."

Erin quickly chimed in, "I will."

Owen replied to Erin, "You should go to bed extra early tonight because you know we have to leave at four thirty tomorrow morning."

Erin nodded and said, "I know. I'm going to go to bed at eight thirty tonight. I set my alarm for four fifteen, so I will be up and ready to go when you leave in the morning."

Owen nodded in agreement.

Erin finished her dinner and helped clear the table. Her mother excused her from doing the dishes so she could finish her homework. Erin's teacher had given her the work she would miss while at the dentist, and Erin was determined to finish everything tonight. Erin completed all her homework by bedtime and quickly changed into her pajamas and brushed her teeth. She crawled into her bed—the lower bed of the bunk beds she shared with Lisa—and fell asleep, looking forward to spending the day with her father.

Erin woke up when the alarm clock chimed. She quickly got dressed, brushed her teeth, and was waiting in the living room by half past four that morning. It was cold and dark outside as Erin hopped into the passenger seat of her dad's car, and they began their journey. Erin fell asleep as her dad drove down the highway and didn't wake up until they entered the Lincoln Tunnel. As they emerged onto the streets of the west side of Manhattan, it was still dark outside.

Owen's first stop was Don's Deli, which was on a side street a few blocks from the garage. Erin waited in the car, and her father returned with two round rolls that were spread generously with at least half an inch of butter, a coffee for him, and an orange juice for Erin. With her buttery breakfast in hand, they entered the New York City sanitation garage on West Fifty-Seventh Street.

Owen parked the car, and they both climbed out with their breakfasts in hand. It was the largest garage Erin had ever seen. Although she had been there many times, each time she visited, she would stare around in awe at how many garbage and sweeper trucks were lined up everywhere.

Erin was instantly greeted by the garage smell she remembered. Of course there was a faint background smell of garbage, but the scent of diesel and engine oil was much more prominent. Erin found the smell pleasant in a way because it brought back a flood of wonderful memories of time spent with her dad.

The garage also had what Erin thought must be the dirtiest floor in the world. The floor was a deep, dark shade of blue-black and was gritty with many years' worth of dirt, oil, and drainage from the garbage trucks. Erin's mother liked everything neat and clean, so Erin laughed to herself, imagining her mother trying to clean this extremely dirty floor.

One of Owen's workers said, "Good morning, Super!" Erin knew that the guys that reported to her dad always called him "Super" instead of saying "Superintendent McGowan." She thought it was cool that everyone called her dad "Super."

It had been almost a year since the last time she had come to work with her dad, so Erin heard several people comment on how tall she had gotten since last time. Erin smiled politely at everyone and followed her father to his office. She immediately took the spare office chair, set up her breakfast on the side of her father's desk, and started eating. Erin loved the fresh rolls from Don's Deli, and she felt a wave of joy as she slowly savored her buttery treat. Her dad finished his breakfast as he reviewed and signed the papers on his desk.

The day trickled by until around two o'clock in the afternoon when her dad took her to the dentist's office. Erin's dentist took x-rays, examined Erin's teeth, and asked questions about the toothache she had. He explained that the pain she had was not a cavity but probably just pain from her molars growing in. Erin was relieved that she was not going to have to undergo the filling procedure she had heard other kids complain about. She had heard that the dentist stuck needles in the patient's mouth and then used a large drill to put a hole in the tooth. Both Erin and her dad left the dentist's office in a great mood and happily began the journey back home.

The ride home took over an hour, so Erin filled the time by asking her dad questions as he drove the car. "Dad, why do you always wear that necklace with the charm on it?"

Owen chuckled as he reached and pulled the necklace out from under his shirt collar. He gently displayed the metal symbol she was reffering to and began, "This is called a triquetra. It has three overlapping shapes that create a symbol with three corners. The triquetra is a Celtic symbol, and our family story is that we are descendents of Celtic druids."

Erin tilted her head and raised her eyebrows as she asked, "What does Celtic mean, and what is a druid?"

Owen continued, "Celts were the people that lived in Ireland thousands of years ago. The word Celtic describes anything that relates to the Celts and their culture. Druids were the healers and leaders of the Celts. They did not have any books or written language, so every generation had to memorize everything they were taught by the older generation."

Erin nodded as she took in this information. Owen paused and said, "This metal triquetra is actually a family heirloom that has been passed down for more generations than I can count. I am not sure if we really are descendents of druids, but I have always heard stories of my mother's past relatives that were considered witches or bizarre for knowing too much."

Erin was nodding when she was distracted by a large billboard advertisement for the Mount Simon Water Park on the side of the highway. Erin quickly asked, "Dad, do remember how this summer we went to the water park with Uncle Sean, Eileen, and Megan? Do you remember how Uncle Sean did the huge belly flop into the pool?"

Owen immediately laughed and said, "Of course, you mean when we were almost kicked out of the water park because Uncle Sean must have saturated everyone sitting around that pool?"

Erin laughed, too, thinking about Uncle Sean and how much fun she had had with her cousins Eileen and Megan. Erin asked, "Can we do that again next summer—have our whole family meet up with Uncle Sean's whole family at the Mount Simon Water Park again?"

Owen smiled and said, "Sure, we'll see if we can set up some time when everyone can go."

Erin smiled and said, "Great, I can't wait!" The water park was fun any day, but it was even better to enjoy it with her cousins, and she hoped that they could repeat the trip next summer.

Erin couldn't have been happier that evening. She didn't have a cavity, and her family would be going to the water park with her cousins the next summer. She fell asleep that night completely content, imagining what her trip to the water park next summer would be like.

2

Fall 2003

Like a scream in the dark, the alarm clock went off. It was 6:15 a.m., and unfortunately it was a weekday. After a few moments, Erin pulled herself together and climbed out of bed. As she looked in the bathroom mirror, she remembered that she should have applied Tri-Luma Cream to the discolored areas on her face before she went to bed. A week ago Erin found out that the freckle smudges that had spread and multiplied on her face were not freckles. They were actually melasma, a discoloration of skin pigmentation and a normal sign of aging also known as liver spots.

Erin was having trouble accepting the symptoms of aging such as melasma and the crow's feet around her eyes because she felt so young, and she was only thirty-five. She quickly applied a few drops of the Tri-Luma Cream to her face and noticed that just a few days of the cream had already began to lighten the discolored areas.

Erin stared in the mirror, and then she turned sideways and sucked in her stomach. She wished that her stomach were flatter. She was five feet seven inches tall and had to diet often to stay in her size six clothes. She gave a resigned sigh and went downstairs to pour the coffee. Her favorite part of the morning was the fifteen minutes she spent with her husband, Dante, in their bathroom, sipping coffee as they got ready to go to work. This was their special time to talk, plan their day, and laugh before they let in the craziness of their daily routines.

It was hard to describe Dante Brusca and the way he made Erin feel. She had grown so close to Dante that she often sensed his presence before he arrived home from work in the evening and felt a palpable loss when he left in the morning—although it had not always been this way. When they were dating, she was usually confused by his mannerisms because he did not express his love with the expected hugs and cuddles of a couple in love. She misunderstood this physical distance as cold, disinterested behavior and was hurt by his lack of interest. Eventually, Erin realized that Dante constantly studied her intensely and kept a distance to avoid smothering her.

He would sometimes go to his desk to pay bills or fix something in the garage, and then he would return and stay within a certain distance of where she was—no matter what she was doing. If she were watching a TV show he didn't like, he would read a magazine or use his laptop at the table nearby. If Erin went upstairs to clean the closet, Dante would find something to do in the next room. Erin eventually realized Dante felt the same comfort she did when they were near each other and the same loss when they were apart.

However, everything with Dante started as a leap of faith. After Erin's first marriage ended in divorce, she had grown very picky about whom she dated. In fact, she was so careful that her brother, David, gave her the nickname Sour Grapes when he grew tired of Erin's negative attitude toward all her potential male suitors in the months that followed her divorce.

Erin's ex-husband was her first love and a fun boyfriend when she was eighteen years old, but they had grown and changed over the years. Erin made the biggest mistake of her life at age twenty-five when she ignored her gut feeling that Tony was not the right person for her and married him out of loyalty. That misplaced loyalty and disregard for her own feelings stung her deeply when she found out two years later that he had been having an affair with her best friend, Katrina. All her immaturity and naïve notions shattered like glass that day when the two people she had trusted the most betrayed her. The agony of her ex-husband's affair left a scar on her emotions that permanently changed her.

Erin did eventually complete the Sour Grapes phase of her life, and she emerged stronger and much more selective in choosing whom she allowed to enter her heart. She found that the hardest part about dating was investing time in a person and then finding out what he was really like when his guard was down and his negative characteristics were exposed. She experienced a bad dating streak and fell for a series of sweet "Dr. Jekylls" who all turned into "Mr. Hydes" a few months into the relationship.

There were ups and downs to being divorced and single at thirty years old. Erin had figured out that her ideal future husband should possess the best features from each of her previous boyfriends when Dante caught her by surprise. He asked her out on a date while they were at a party. Erin and Dante had been friends when they had worked in the same hospital several years before and occasionally kept in touch, but Erin had reservations about Dante and kept her distance for many reasons.

Dante was divorced as she was, but he had a daughter tying him to his ex-wife, Susan, and Erin was not sure she could deal with that type of complication. It was actually the fact that he had a daughter that prompted her to say no the first time Dante asked her on a date. Besides, she knew Dante was a good man since they were friends, but he was not a complete blend of the best features of her former beaus. He just wasn't the dream man she was looking for.

Dante was the son of Italian immigrants and had a wonderful, modest disposition—despite his attractive physical appearance. He was a little over six feet tall and was blessed with beautiful Roman facial features and pale olive skin. He had prominent eyebrows, beautiful big emerald-green eyes, and a strong chin—a combination that could grab most women's attention with a glance. Erin thought that his most attractive feature was that he was unaware of the effect he had on women.

Erin didn't think Dante was her type, though. He was the nerdy, brainy-doctor type, and she was generally attracted to "bad boys." But by the time Erin turned thirty and had dealt with her heart being broken too many times, she realized that she had to grow up and stop dating "bad boys." She eventually said yes to Dante.

Erin would never forget her first date with Dante for many reasons. Dante made a very memorable appearance when he came to pick her up from her apartment in Hoboken, New Jersey. He drove up and parked his Harley Davidson motorcycle in front of her apartment building. Erin had never seen him ride his motorcycle, and she remembered staring at his black leather jacket, motorcycle riding boots, and helmet. She even let out a little gasp when he took off his helmet and she realized that he looked like a real bad ass in his motorcycle gear. As they walked to the restaurant for dinner, she had a whole new appreciation for Dante.

Unlike most first dates, Erin was totally comfortable chatting and sharing information without worrying about how Dante would perceive her. They ate delicious food, shared a wonderful bottle of wine, and enjoyed a crisp, beautiful walk on the way back to Erin's place. She was a little nervous that the situation would become awkward when they said good night. Erin had decided that she would just say good-bye with a hug. As Erin was mentally confirming her decision, Dante leaned in and surprised her with a kiss.

Erin had read numerous romance novels and thought that a magical first kiss was purely fiction...until that night. She was thirty years old and had previously experienced wonderful, passionate kissing, but her first kiss with Dante changed her life. It was at that moment that she realized they were meant to be together. That first kiss was the first step to seriously dating and eventually marrying Dante.

Currently, they were still considered newlyweds because they had only been married for a year and a half. However, Sandra, Dante's fifteen-year-old daughter, lived with them full time, and most days

Dante and Erin operated as if they had been married for many years. They shared the parenting responsibilities, including chauffeuring Sandra to school, doling out consequences for bad grades, and enduring the nonstop mood swings of a teenage girl.

Erin, Dante, and Sandra lived in a three-bedroom, center-hall colonial home in North Haledon, New Jersey. Dante had told Erin that he had considered opting for more of a bachelor-type apartment after his divorce, but he wanted to create the setting of a warm, typical home for Sandra to visit. It was an expensive option that forced Dante deeper into debt, but it was for the best in the end when Sandra chose to come live with Erin and Dante full time.

Erin showered, dressed, and applied her makeup as she chatted with Dante. As their morning coffee ritual drew to a close at seven o'clock, Erin said good-bye to her husband while he was trying to pick out a tie to wear. She put on a pair of earrings, grabbed her purse, gathered up their coffee cups, and walked downstairs toward the kitchen.

Before Erin could even say good morning, Sandra quickly blurted out, "*We're late!*"

Erin controlled her first impulse to yell back and calmly stated, "It is seven a.m. School doesn't start until seven thirty, and it is only a five-minute drive."

With a frustrated sigh, Sandra reminded Erin that she liked to be at school early, before 7:10 a.m. Erin quickly grabbed her lunch from the refrigerator and her jacket from the hall closet and climbed into the car with her completely disgruntled fifteen-year-old stepdaughter.

Sandra was truly a good kid. She never smoked, did drugs, or joined in the underage drinking parties her classmates planned. Erin actually admired Sandra's strength because she was a teenager who was able to stay strong against peer pressure in a time when most teens were easily persuaded into trouble. However, Erin was having difficulty focusing on Sandra's positive traits this morning.

Watching Sandra stamp her way to the car in frustration reminded Erin that moments like this made her question the choice she had made. Erin believed that Sandra loved her and that Sandra's be-havior was a normal phase that would pass. Erin had been recently reassured that her assessment was correct when she saw her fifteen-year-old niece, Maggie, treat Lisa the same horrible way. Erin loved Maggie and Lisa, and she was not happy to see her niece's behavior; however, it was reassuring to know that it was not unusual for a teen-age girl to treat her mother horribly at this age and that the issue was not that she was Sandra's stepmom.

Erin and Dante had nicknamed Sandra's fifteenth year the "alien phase." Erin remembered and regretted the things she had said to her own mother when she was fifteen, but it was still hard to deal with a fifteen-year-old who treated her like an idiot. Thus, on mornings like this, Erin tried to focus on the fact that this phase would even-tually pass. Erin fully concentrated on this theory while she weaved through the school buses and cars to drop Sandra at the front door of Manchester High School. Sandra jumped out of the car, barked a good-bye, slammed the car door, and stormed up to the entrance.

Erin took a deep breath and scanned the radio stations to find something cheery to listen to so she could get her mind off Sandra's teenage angst and continue the day more positively. By a quarter to eight, Erin was driving down the main road of the industrial park where Kaso Pharmaceuticals was located. Her office building was the last one in a row of a dozen identical four-story buildings. Erin pulled into the first row of the parking lot at the rear of the building. She scanned her badge to open the door at the back entrance, entered the building, and walked over to a section of cubicles on the south-ern-facing wall of the first floor. Although it was early, Molly was al-ready at her own desk in the cube next to Erin's. Her friend peeked over the wall dividing their cubicles and smiled.

Molly worked on the same study team as Erin. She was the most positive person Erin knew and was her closest friend at work. She was twenty-seven years old and was one of those amazing people who got along with everyone. Molly was five feet two inches tall, with long, straight, auburn hair that fell past her shoulders. Her twinkling sea-blue eyes added warmth to her welcoming smile; it was no wonder that everyone wanted to be her friend.

As a natural introvert, Erin was the complete opposite of Molly and would have been exhausted if she tried to socialize with everyone in the company. Erin had a tendency to chat briefly with the people on her study team and then throw herself into her work for most of the day. Molly was sort of Erin's ambassador, and Erin relied on her to keep the departmental social links alive.

Erin and Molly worked on Kaso Pharmaceuticals' clinical trial of a drug for pancreatic cancer. An earlier clinical trial with two hundred patient participants who had pancreatic cancer showed that 95 percent of the patients who received the new drug were cured. The excitement was palpable, and the company was intent on finishing the current clinical trial and getting this medication out into the world so that it could start saving lives. The majority of the Kaso employees were also aware of the tight study time lines, and everyone was counting the days left to finish the clinical trial, submit the results to the FDA, and get the drug to patients that needed it.

Molly quickly chirped, "Good morning!"

Erin couldn't help smiling back and returned, "Good morning. How are you?"

Molly was smiling ear to ear and replied, "Really good. Tonight I am taking Jack out for his birthday, and he doesn't know it yet, but I was able to get reservations at that new Portuguese restaurant, Chapa, in Tribeca! He has been talking about how some of his friends went there a few weeks ago and how much they loved it. I can't wait to see his face when I tell him!"

"Our neighbors were just raving about Chapa. You have to let me know if it's worth the trip into the city or not," Erin responded.

"Of course. I am skipping lunch today to make sure I have plenty of room for a nice big dinner."

Molly and Jack had been dating for over a year, and Jack seemed like the perfect match for Molly. Erin was genuinely happy for both of them.

Erin and Molly settled into their routine of managing their study sites by answering e-mails, reviewing documents, and making phone calls. About an hour later, Erin finished her coffee and stood up to go to the kitchen to get a refill when she heard Molly gasp and cry out, "Oh no!"

Erin saw Molly staring at the cell phone in her hand and asked, "What happened?"

Molly's cheeks were flushed, and she rubbed her forehead and half laughed as she replied, "I am such an idiot. I just sent a text to Jack saying, 'I just want to let you know that I am thinking about you and that I love you very much.' The problem is that after I hit Send, I realized that I had texted my cousin Jackie by accident!"

Erin burst out laughing as Molly's cell phone beeped, indicating she had received a message.

Molly looked down at her cell phone and continued, "My cousin Jackie just replied, 'Either I am the most loved cousin in the world or this message was meant for Jack.'"

Erin was laughing so hard she had tears in her eyes as she imaged how funny it must have been to receive that love message from a cousin. Molly's face was bright red with embarrassment; however, she was also laughing at herself. They both got up and continued chuckling as they walked to the pantry for coffee.

The rest of Erin's day was uneventful, and she followed her normal routine of picking up Sandra from cheerleading practice and stopping at the grocery store to buy food for dinner on her way home. Erin had just finished cooking the chicken when Dante walked into the kitchen, gave her a kiss, and asked, "What's for dinner?"

Erin responded, "We are having baked chicken, steamed broccoli, and rice."

She felt that familiar warm wave of love as she watched Dante smile and say, "Smells good! Let's eat."

After Sandra, Dante, and Erin ate dinner, Dante helped Erin do the dishes, and Sandra went upstairs to her bedroom to finish her homework. By the time they finished putting away the dishes, it was almost nine o'clock. Erin went upstairs and began her bedtime routine of washing her face and flossing and brushing her teeth. As she walked into her bedroom, she paused in front of the bookshelf and began scanning the titles of the paperback books for something she might not have read recently. As she reached for a book that looked like a nice, steamy romantic story, she brushed the double picture frame that was angled in front of the books and knocked it over.

As Erin righted the frame, she looked at both of the three-by-five-inch photos from her childhood in the 1970s. The photo on the left was of her father and Erin standing in the front yard of her childhood home. Erin's father was dressed for work in his green uniform pants and white dress shirt, and ten-year-old Erin was wearing her favorite white T-shirt with the yellow smiley face on it. The second photo was taken a few months later, and it captured Erin with her dad and her Uncle Sean, along with her cousins Eileen and Megan, all standing arm in arm in front of the sign for Mount Simon Water Park. Erin stared at the photos. She quickly calculated that the pictures were taken over twenty-five years before. The photos had a yellowish-orange hue to them, but Erin smiled as she remembered the days both photos were taken.

A loud crash from downstairs snapped her out of her thoughts of the past. She walked into the hallway and shouted downstairs, "Is everything OK?"

"Yeah, I just dropped a bowl," Dante replied. Erin went downstairs and helped him sweep up the remaining pieces. Dante settled into the sofa and clicked on the TV with the remote.

Erin yawned and said, "I'm beat. I think I'm going to go to sleep."

Dante looked up and said, "OK, I'll be up in a few minutes; I just want to catch the score of the Jets game."

Erin walked back upstairs and then settled into bed. She pulled up the blankets, took a deep breath, and relaxed her muscles. She thought about how fast time raced by and felt a little nostalgic. It felt like just yesterday that she was a child, and now she had this full life where she barely had time to catch her breath.

Erin thought about how things were when she was born in 1968 and wished that she could go back to the simple life of her childhood. She wondered if any child ever appreciates how wonderful life is before experiencing the burdens of adulthood. She focused on her breathing as she felt herself falling asleep. Just then Dante slipped into bed and gently took her hand. They fell asleep together, still holding hands.

3

As with most of her dreams, Erin had been at the place she was dreaming about before and recognized it as the New York City sanitation garage where her dad used to work. It was a dark, sunless room when the garage doors were closed, with the only illumination coming from large, hanging florescent lights.

This dream was weird, as were all Erin's dreams. She was looking down at the gritty black floor of the garage as she pedaled a bike that was a hybrid of the reclining bicycle she exercised on at the gym and the big-wheel bike she rode as a kid. A red balloon that was tied to the back of the bike lazily followed her. She breathed in the familiar garage smell and pedaled across the dark floor, heading toward the side door. In this dream Erin had the strongest sensation that she had to be somewhere, and she was moving with a purpose to get there.

When she reached the side door, the urgent feeling grew stronger. She stood up and opened the door. Erin was immediately blinded by the bright sunlight, but after a few seconds, her vision slowly returned. Erin stepped outside and gasped when she saw that *everything had changed.*

Erin still had the strong feeling that she had to be somewhere, but the cloudiness that filled Erin's peripheral vision in all her dreams had dissolved, and she was seeing the street exactly as if she were wide awake. The sunny street was incredibly clear—more real look-ing than any other dream she had experienced.

Erin was standing on the sidewalk in shock, bathed in beautiful bright sunlight, when the urgency to get somewhere returned. Erin tried to identify her surroundings to help her figure out which way she should go. That was when she noticed a man standing several feet away on the sidewalk. Perhaps he might be able to help her find her way, she thought in relief. The man was an average height, thin, and with brown hair. He was wearing the dark-green slacks and light-green dress shirt of an NYC sanitation uniform.

As he turned to her, she noticed he was young, and she guessed he was in his late twenties or early thirties. His facial expression was distorted, and he seemed distracted for a second and rubbed his ears as if he heard something unpleasant. He had round cheeks with fair skin and warm, welcoming hazel eyes. Then the realization hit Erin like a ton of bricks—it was her *dad*! This was not the father she knew, but a younger, thinner version that she had seen in old pictures taken before she was born. A tidal wave of emotion hit her as she stood a few feet in front of this version of her dad that she had never seen in person before.

Erin's father had grown up in the 1940s and 1950s, and he had never lost that innocence and generosity of the earlier part of the century. True to form, although she was staring at her dad with her mouth open in a state of shock, he looked at her with genuine con-cern and asked, "Are you OK?"

Erin was not OK. She couldn't talk. The dream felt so real, but why was she looking at a young Owen? And if she knew him, why did it seem that he didn't know her? She finally managed to whisper, "It's me, Erin."

His next statement confirmed her impression when he said, "Nice to meet you, Erin; I'm Owen."

Erin felt like she was going to explode with amazement. This could not be happening, yet she had never felt so awake and aware. Thank God her dad had always been an easygoing, sweet person because, instead of running from her, he remained silent for an extra moment to give her time to recover. Erin was too dumbfounded to ask where she was, the original reason she had approached him.

In that same moment, another young man with a blue cap walked past her and gave her dad a slap on the back, followed by a hug, and with a laugh said, "You're buying lunch, right?" Erin could not see this man's face, but she could still see her dad's face, and it was filled with joy at the sight of this other man. Right after the hug and slap on the back, the young man turned around to see what her dad was looking at, and Erin experienced another shock. It was a younger version of her Uncle Sean. Uncle Sean was wearing his blue NYC fireman's uniform and cap. He gave Erin a polite nod, took a quick look at his watch, and ushered her dad down the street, reminding him that he had to be back at the firehouse at one o'clock.

Erin's dad gave her an apologetic look over his shoulder and let himself be ushered down the street. He looked so happy to be with his brother. As they walked away, Erin's brain started working. Uncle Sean had been her dad's closest sibling and his best friend, but he had died of colon cancer when Erin was nineteen. Erin's dad had taken early retirement to spend the last three months of Uncle Sean's life at his bedside, caring for him as he slowly died from the malignant tumors that ate away at his body. The day Erin's uncle Sean died, part of her dad died, and he had never seemed truly happy again.

Erin had just witnessed the love between the two brothers, and she was so overcome with joy for the bond they shared and sorrow for what their future held that she began to sob uncontrollably, moaning and gasping for air. She woke up from the dream crying. She lay in bed next to her husband and then slowly got out of bed and walked to the bathroom, completely aware that something bizarre had just happened. Erin couldn't help thinking about how much her dad loved her uncle Sean and how much he must miss him every day.

Erin would never forget visiting Uncle Sean the summer after her freshman year at college. She had been recovering from having her wisdom teeth removed at the time of her visit. Uncle Sean was in the final terminal stages of his cancer, and the doctors had inserted an experimental chemotherapy pump in his back that delivered chemotherapy continuously. At that point the cancer had spread everywhere, and he was no longer able to keep food down. Yet, Uncle Sean was worried about how Erin was feeling after her oral surgery and was happy to see that she was not in pain and doing better. Erin wondered how someone who felt that horrible could be concerned about his niece's minor surgery. But that was typical of her uncle Sean. He died a month later. Erin still missed him terribly, and this dream just reminded her of the depth of her family's loss.

Erin washed her face with cold water, dried it with a towel, and stared at herself in the bathroom mirror. Her eyelids were swollen and puffy from crying, and her eyes appeared a much lighter shade of blue against her red, swollen lids. Her pale skin looked almost translucent, which only exaggerated the dark circles under her eyes. With a sigh she noticed that her long brown hair was starting to wave, even though she had straightened it before she went to bed.

She looked horrible after her crying episode. Erin went back to bed and lay there for what felt like a long time. She could not stop thinking about her dream experience. Everything had been so crystal clear and real that she could not shake her unease. Finally, she fell back to sleep.

4

Dante's parents were poor Italian immigrants that worked tirelessly to survive and acheive their American dream of buying a home and putting their son through college and medical school. Dante's parents did not have time for frivolous activites or beliefs and in turn Dante frowned upon anything that was not based on factual evidence. He was not open-minded about dreams or superstitions, so she knew he was not going to be that receptive to hearing about her dream that morning. However, it was too fresh, and she couldn't hold back. She blurted out some of the details of her dream and described how real it had felt. Just as she could have predicted, Dante was not impressed or interested in hearing about a weird dream.

Erin dropped the subject and went through her normal morning routine of getting ready. Dante had taken Sandra to school, so Erin had a peaceful drive to work. As she accelerated down the entrance ramp to the highway, a glance at the dashboard reminded Erin that she needed gas, and she quickly recalculated how much time a stop at the gas station was going to cost her.

Grudgingly, Erin pulled off the highway into the gas station. Her goal was to fuel up quickly and be back on the highway before the morning rush-hour traffic got too bad. While the attendant filled the gas tank, Erin ran into the station's store to buy a lotto ticket. She knew she had a better chance of being hit by lightning then of winning the $100 million jackpot, but she couldn't resist the temptation and the chance to dream of a life where she didn't have to work so hard and run around so much.

A big smile broke across Erin's face as she walked back to her car and saw that the gas pump had stopped and she could be back on the road right away. Just then a blond-haired, blue-eyed young man wearing a black suit stepped in front of her and blocked her path. Without skipping a beat, this man looked at her and said, "Erin, please listen to me, and don't say anything!"

Erin was confused and searched the man's face, wondering if she had ever met him before.

"We know you had your first experience last night," he said, "and you need to know some things right away."

Erin stuttered, "Wh-what are you talking about?"

The blond stranger said, "You are older than most for your first time, but you must know some things right away. There are rules. The most important rule is that you must not tell anyone what happened! It is too much for the public to comprehend, and the consequences of the public finding out would be disastrous!"

Erin could barely get a word in but managed, "What are you talking about?"

The blond stranger continued. "Last night, or actually early this morning, we know you traveled to 1968 and spoke with your father. You really should try to avoid communicating and interacting on your dream travel at this point because you are so new to it and don't know what you're doing."

Erin thought her head might explode trying to comprehend this whole bizarre experience. She broke away and almost ran back to her car. She gave the attendant cash and jammed the key into the ignition. She sped out of the gas station and, in the process, almost got into a car accident with a tractor-trailer as she merged back onto the highway.

Who was that man, and how did he know her name and what she was dreaming about last night? Questions raced through her head for the rest of her commute to work. However, those thoughts were quickly squashed when she walked into her office building and almost collided with Debra at the entrance.

Debra said in a panicked voice, "Thank God, you're here! Molly is in the middle of a crisis, and I think she is about to have an anxiety attack!"

Debra was the department administrative assistant and was like a second mother to most of the people who worked in Erin's department. She had been born and raised in Texas and had the sweetest, most caring nature of anyone in the office. She was constantly going out of her way to help everyone and expected absolutely nothing in return. Debra was in her early forties with reddish-brown, chin-length hair and compassionate cocoa-brown eyes. She was five feet ten inches tall and very slender. She was one of those people who could eat anything she wanted to and was blessed with a fast metabolism that kept her at a size zero. Erin sprinted past Debra to Molly's desk.

Molly's face was red, and her eyes were shiny with tears. As Erin raced up, Molly blurted out, "We have a problem with the randomization schedule!"

Erin quickly comprehended the impact that this could have on the enrollment in their clinical trial and pushed the weird interaction at the gas station out of her mind.

"Why is this schedule so important?" Debra asked.

Erin quickly explained. "To be able to prove that our study drug works and is safe, some patients receive the drug and some receive a placebo, which is also known as a sugar pill. If the patients, the doctors at the study sites, or members of our team knew who was receiving the drug or placebo, it would compromise the study.

"For example, if a doctor knew a patient was on a placebo, he or she might not report any problems the patient was having because the doctor would know the problems were not from the study drug. That would be really bad because the best way to know if a drug is safe is to compare the problems reported by the patients on the study drug with the problems reported by the patients on the placebo.

"Thus, we use a computer program to randomly select whether the patient is assigned to the drug or a placebo. This information is kept secret from us at Kaso, and it is also kept secret from the doctors and the patients until after the study is over. When the drug/placebo assignment is kept a secret like this, the study is called a blinded study. The computer program that randomly selects drug or placebo assignments is called a randomization schedule."

Debra nodded and said, "OK, now I understand."

Erin continued, "Our Kaso team cannot work directly with the randomization schedule because if we see the drug/placebo assignments, they would no longer be a secret. The worst part is that without this randomization schedule working, no patients can be enrolled in the study!"

Debra sympathetically nodded, and as she departed, she added, "I understand. Please let me know if I can do anything to help."

Erin loved being part of groundbreaking research that could save thousands of lives, but she did not like mornings like this. She quickly started helping Molly solve the problem in the randomization schedule and keep the damage to enrollment to a minimum. Erin was upset, but Molly was horrified because deep down she always felt inadequate in her position.

Molly's brother-in-law, Ronan McKenna, also worked at Kaso and was a study director on a clinical trial for a drug for male-pattern baldness. Ronan's clinical trial had recently been completed, and it had made him a star because it looked like his team had found the first medication that completely stopped hair loss and regrew previously lost hair. Although Molly was fully qualified for her position, some people still murmured that she was hired because her brother-in-law was part of senior management. Erin knew that Molly was a wonderful addition to the team and was ready and willing to do anything to help her.

Erin had a feeling that the negative things people said about Molly were based on the general public reaction to any person associated with Ronan McKenna. Ronan had slick-backed black hair, a fake tan all year long, and teeth that were so white and Hollywood perfect that everyone could tell that they were veneers. Ronan had a reputation of being a shallow, career-climbing jerk who was not afraid to step on anyone to get ahead. Company legends circulated about how many people he had "thrown under the bus" when things went wrong rather than owning up to his own mistakes. Most people were afraid to work for him because it was just a matter of time until something went wrong and someone would be fired for Ronan's mistake. However, Erin didn't blame Molly for being related to Ronan. In fact she felt sorry for her, and she thought Molly was a wonderful person.

Skipping breakfast, inhaling lunch in one minute at her desk, and experiencing a few hours of heartburn did pay off because, with lots of phone calls and favors called in, Molly and Erin were able to solve the problem, keep the study on schedule, and maintain the study time lines. Erin had lost track of time until she received a text message from Sandra at half past five: *Are you or my dad going to pick me up?* With a quick good-bye to Molly, Erin was out the door and starting her evening routine of battling traffic to pick up Sandra, finding something to cook at the grocery store, and getting dinner on the table.

Navigating the rush-hour traffic and mentally figuring out what she should make for dinner tonight kept Erin's mind busy until she passed a gas station and was reminded of the unsettling incident that had taken place that morning. Just then her cell phone rang, and with the press of a button, she was relieved to hear Dante's voice say, "Hello, I have two patients left to see, and I can't really talk right now, but can you pick up Sandra from cheerleading practice?"

Erin replied, "No problem, I'm already on my way right now." Erin then quickly added, "Oh, remind me to tell you something that happened to me today when you get home later."

"OK, love you. See you in about an hour. Bye," Dante said as he hung up.

Erin pressed the End button on her cell phone as she pulled into the Manchester High School driveway. Sandra, wearing her high school cheerleading outfit, was waiting, and she quickly jumped into the passenger's seat. She was clutching her iPod and had her earbuds in her ears, listening to music. She buckled her seat belt and gave Erin a quick wave.

After a long day like this, Erin enjoyed the rest of the silent drive to the grocery store. When Erin pulled into the store parking lot, Sandra—earbuds still in place—signaled that she wanted to stay in the car by raising her eyebrows and pointing at her seat. Erin agreed with a nod, turned off the car, and locked the doors after she stepped out.

It was the day before Thanksgiving, and the grocery store was festively decorated with Thanksgiving decorations. Tall bundles of dry corn stalks framed the entrance and exit doors and silly smiling paper turkeys were taped to the windows and walls. Each grocery aisle was packed with people buying last-minute items for the holiday meal. Erin quickly decided that she would just grab sashimi and sushi rolls from the seafood counter. It was a little pricey, but it required no cooking or cleaning pots and pans, and after her stressful day, that was too tempting for Erin to pass up.

Erin navigated over to the self-service checkout and quickly scanned her items and paid with her credit card. She was briskly walking out of the store when she almost knocked over a woman in front of the exit doors. Erin immediately slowed her pace and patiently waited for the woman, who seemed in no particular hurry, to proceed ahead of her.

The woman was average height with a curvy, robust figure. She had light-olive skin; deep-chocolate, almond-shaped eyes; and a chin-length, hazelnut-brown bob of wavy hair. Erin guessed that the woman was probably in her midsixties. They finally exited the store, and just as Erin thought she could pass her, the woman dropped her purse.

"Oh no!" she said as the contents spilled out on the ground.

Erin was in a hurry but knew that it would be rude not to help. She quickly put down her grocery bag and bent to help the woman gather her items when she realized the woman was staring intently at her.

"Thank you, Erin, but could I talk to you alone for five minutes?" the woman asked. This was the second time in one day that a complete stranger was addressing Erin by her first name, and it more than scared her. The mysterious woman noticed the fear in her expression and said, "Please do not be alarmed. My name is Anna, and I really need to talk to you."

Erin was numbed by this interaction, and she slowly followed the woman to an emptier area of the parking lot.

The woman quietly said, "Again, please do not be alarmed. Like I said, my name is Anna, and I mean no harm. I am here to help you. I know that Steve met you this morning and gave you a lot of information before you were ready to hear it."

"Steve? Do you mean the man in the gas station this morning?" Erin said.

Anna continued. "Yes, he can sometimes be abrupt and does not realize that this kind of information can be hard to understand at first."

Erin was speechless for the second time that day and could only nod.

"I know this is new and hard to understand, Erin, so I will wait until you are ready to talk about it."

Anna handed Erin a piece of paper with a phone number on it and said, "Just call me when you're ready to talk, but please do not tell anyone about this. It's very important that you do not share anything you have learned today from Steve or from me with anyone else. Do you understand?"

Erin muttered a yes and stumbled back to her car, her mind racing with questions. She stuffed the piece of paper with Anna's phone number into her purse as she sat down in the car. Thankfully, Sandra was still engrossed in her music and did not see what had just happened. She simply acknowledged Erin getting back in the car with a nod.

Erin pushed through the rest of the evening and night, completely distracted by what had happened that day. Her anxiety grew as she moved through her regular nighttime activities of washing her face and brushing her teeth. What if something weird was going to happen again? It took her a while to get to sleep, but she finally fell into a deep, peaceful, dream-free slumber.

Erin woke up the next day feeling refreshed and a little silly for letting herself get so worked up the day before. She piled into the car with Dante and Sandra to go to her brother's house for Thanksgiving dinner. Erin convinced herself that Steve and Anna must be part of some type of scam or joke, and she was embarrassed for falling for it. She figured this exact scenario would probably show up in a forwarded mass e-mail warning women of a scam. She could just imagine the warning to avoid people who seemed to know your name because they were involved in identity theft or could figure out a way to charge calls to your phone line. Erin was happy to put the whole thing out of her mind for good.

Dante and Erin dropped Sandra off at her mom's house, and after about an hour-long drive, they arrived at David's house. Erin was elated when the first person who greeted them at the door with a big hug was her father. Owen was in his midsixties, and his brown hair had changed to salt-and-pepper. He still kept the same cropped style he had worn ever since he had enlisted in the army at age eighteen. He was about six feet tall with an average build and the potbelly common to men his age. Owen was dressed in jeans with a dark-blue sweatshirt, and he had a huge grin on his face. Erin knew that, out of his three kids, she was his favorite and that her dad absolutely adored Dante.

Erin's mom, Helen, was right by her dad's side and was smiling and shaking her head as Owen started chatting with Dante about a new bill that was being voted on in Congress. Helen laughed as she said, "Let them take their coats off, Owen, before you start chewing their ears off!"

Helen was petite, but she had large, steel-blue eyes that went with her strong personality. She had kept her hair in the same short, feathered style for as long as Erin could remember, and over the years it had changed from honey-blond to silver.

Everyone else in the family was already there when they arrived. David and his wife, Kelly, were busy prepping and cooking together in the kitchen when they walked in and exchanged hugs. Erin's sister, Lisa, and her husband, Bob, were sitting at the kitchen counter island and quickly got in line to share warm hugs.

Erin's niece, Maggie, popped her head over the top of her laptop and yelled, "Aunt Erin!" Then she joined in the line for hugs. It was a great start to a holiday, and it quickly progressed to a lot of overeating while sharing stories and news about friends and family. Erin noted that Dante had quickly adapted to a typical Irish American family gathering, where the food might not be as good as it was with his Italian family, but the mood was so positive and happy that you couldn't help having a great time.

At some point after dessert, Erin joined her father in the family room and sat down next to him on the couch to watch TV. Everyone else had found a spot to hang out or a bed to fall into in the turkey-induced coma that had resulted from the feast. As they watched TV together, Erin's curiosity got the best of her, and she asked, "Dad, when you were working as a foreman, did you ever get the chance to meet Uncle Sean and go out for lunch or anything?"

Owen answered, "Yes, when I first became a foreman, I was put on the day shift at the same time Uncle Sean was working the day shift at a firehouse only a few blocks away. However, right after you were born, Joe McCarthy retired, and I had to switch back to the night shift. I stayed on that shift for the next five years until I was promoted to superintendent. By the time I came back to the day shift, Uncle Sean had changed to a firehouse in Queens, and we were too far apart to get together for lunch at that point.

"So to answer your question, I think we only got the chance to get together for lunch that one time when I met the woman that you were named after."

Erin felt a jolt of fear at what she thought she heard her father saying. Erin stuttered, "Wha…what?"

Owen looked slightly embarrassed as he said, "Oh, I guess I never told you about how I met that woman when I was waiting for Uncle Sean. Well, I was standing on the street when I noticed this beautiful woman with long brown hair and big blue eyes staring at me. She seemed confused or lost or something, and I thought she was from another country because she just stared at me and didn't speak. Then she said her name was Erin.

"It's funny because she told me her name as if I were supposed to already know her or something. Needless to say, I thought she was very attractive, so when you were born, I told your mother that we should name you Erin. It was a long time ago, and my memory might be wrong, but I think you grew up to look a lot like her. Maybe it has something to do with the name, or…maybe my mind is going these days. Who knows?"

Erin's mind could not comprehend what was going on. She blurted out, "Mom said that she named me Erin because Nanny wanted one of your kids to have an Irish name, and you picked out Erin!"

Erin's dad laughed and responded, "Well, of course I said that to your mother. Do you think she wanted to hear that I was naming you after a woman I met on the street? I don't think I ever told your mother what really inspired your name, so if you wouldn't mind, let's keep this between us."

Erin sat dumbfounded, trying to understand how her father could have described her dream from the other night so perfectly. She had always heard the story that Nanny, her dad's mother, had picked out her name, and Erin had accepted the explanation. What did it mean that her dream from yesterday had actually taken place thirty-five years ago? How could that be? It was just too impossible to understand.

Owen noticed her expression and said, "Sorry, sweetie, if I knew this would upset you this much, I would have never brought it up."

Erin tried to smile and make light of it. "No, Dad, it's not that. I'm preoccupied about something else. Don't worry about it; I'll get over it."

Erin didn't want to upset her dad and tried to hide her feelings from everyone else. She pushed everything from her mind and was able to get through the rest of the evening without drawing too much attention to herself.

Erin didn't let her mind wander until they were driving home. Was it really some kind of dream travel like the guy, Steve, from the gas station said the other day? Why was this happening to her? Would it happen again? Erin's mind was racing with questions she couldn't answer.

Her thoughts were too much to deal with, and the only resolution Erin could think of was to call Anna. By the time she got home, Erin had concluded that she would call the woman from the grocery store first thing the next morning. Erin's stomach roiled until she fell asleep, terrified that she was going to have another unexplainable experience while she was sleeping.

5

Erin had fallen asleep terrified that she was going to travel in time and do something that would be detrimental in some way or another. After a night of tossing and turning, she felt exhausted the next morning when she woke up. She was relieved at the thought that she would have answers today after she called Anna.

Around eight o'clock Erin waved good-bye to Dante and Sandra from the doorway as they drove toward the mall to brave the Black Friday crowds in search of holiday bargains. The mall excursion bought Erin the time she needed. She picked up the phone and dialed the number on the piece of paper that Anna had given her two days before. After two rings Anna picked up the phone with a warm hello. Erin hesitated but then quickly explained that she was ready to hear more information. After a short exchange, Anna agreed to meet Erin in town at a place called Joe's Coffee Shop at eleven o'clock.

Joe's Coffee Shop was a small local bakery and café that was trying to keep up with the mega coffee shop chains that sold cups of coffee for five dollars. "Trying to keep up" was a good way to describe the blend of old and new. The owners had painted the walls a stylish green and had listed the coffee menu on chalkboards but had kept the circa 1950s tables and chairs.

Erin was so relieved to finally find out more information about what was going on that she actually greeted Anna with a warm smile when she arrived at the coffee shop. However, another part of Erin was terrified about what she might find out. To an outsider it must have looked like a casual meeting of two friends over a cup coffee, but Erin felt the opposite of relaxed and casual.

The women settled into a table in the corner of the coffee shop, and Erin was relieved when Anna started the conversation. "Why don't we start by you telling me about the dream you had the other night," Anna suggested.

Erin was grateful for the prompt, and she spilled the whole story of the dream and followed it with an explanation of what her father had told her on Thanksgiving Day.

Erin found it comforting that Anna was not surprised. She was pleasantly relieved that Anna appeared almost bored as she listened to the most shocking experience that Erin had ever had. When Erin finished her story, Anna paused, sighed, and said, "Are you ready to hear why this is happening?"

With a hesitant nod, Erin braced herself.

"Everything we see in life isn't as easily explained as we think it is." Anna told her stories and theories that Erin would have never believed previously but that didn't seem so farfetched after what she had experienced in the past week. Anna explained that certain people are born with the gift of dream travel.

"Dream travel is time travel, except it occurs while the dream traveler is sleeping. Very few people are born with this gift," Anna said. She gently added, "Erin, your experience this week confirmed that you are a dream traveler."

Seeing Erin's shocked expression, Anna asked Erin if she had ever heard a ringing in her ears. Erin slowly responded with a hesitant, "Uh...yes."

Anna patiently explained that anytime a person hears a ringing sound, a dream traveler is present in his or her environment. Erin quickly scanned her mind to try to recount times in the past when she had heard ringing in her ears. She was in awe as she considered the possibility that dream travelers had been around her without her knowledge.

However, the most frightening part of Anna's conversation was the warning regarding Terrents. "There is a group of people called Terrents, and just as you have the gift of dream travel, they have the gift of being able to hijack a dream traveler," Anna said. "Terrents have harnessed this gift and have figured out how to manipulate dream travelers to travel to a time they want to observe or interact in. Just as dream travelers can think of the time they want to travel to and arrive there, if Terrents physically touch dream travelers in the dream-travel process, they can move to the time they want by holding the dream traveler and concentrating on the time they want to travel to. Once they both arrive, the Terrent is free to wander around and affect life at that time until the dream traveler wakes up."

Erin gulped her cappuccino a little too fast and coughed as her tongue and throat burned. She hesitated and quietly said, "How would I know if a Terrent is around when I dream travel?"

"Well, sometimes there is no warning; however, a lot of dream travelers have reported that they experienced a feeling of foreboding prior to the attack. If you experience this, you have to try and wake up prior to a Terrent hijacking your dream travel."

Erin had a question that had been bothering her. "Anna, Steve said that I am rather old for this to be happening for the first time. What did he mean?"

"Yes, it's unusual for this to start at the age of thirty-five," Anna responded. "Has anything unusual happened in your life recently?"

Erin quickly responded, "No, everything has been pretty quiet recently."

Anna continued, "Well, usually dream travel starts when a person goes through puberty; however, sometimes it's delayed until something significant happens or someone is under tremendous stress.

"I'm not sure why you started your dream travel so late, but you should be fine." Anna added, "We know there were a few dream travelers on your father's side of the family, but it was over a hundred years ago."

Just when Erin thought she couldn't take in any more information, Anna offered one more aspect. "There is a very unique and rare type of dream traveler called a Garan. There are only six known Garans right now. Garans have the ability to summon other dream travelers into their own dream travel. In addition, they have the ability to dream travel not only back in time, as you can, but they can also go forward into the future. The Garans are also in charge of the Dream Travel Council."

Anna continued, "All the Garans are stationed in different places throughout the world to cover all the time zones of normal sleep cycles. In addition, Garans have the ability to sense changes in the time continuum when a dream traveler causes a change in history. When you interacted with your father the other night, Sienna sensed this new fluctuation, and we began tracking you right away."

Erin had a thousand questions in her head, but she could not handle any more information. She yearned to just go home and take a nap and try to digest all this information. Anna sensed her exhaustion and approached the next delicate topic cautiously.

"There is mandatory training for all new dream travelers, which you will have to undergo right away."

Erin started shaking her head no and quickly interjected, "I don't have any time right now. I'm superbusy at work."

Anna smiled and explained, "The training takes place while you are sleeping. Sienna, the Garan, will summon you and will perform all your training during your normal sleep hours. You will have to fall asleep by ten o'clock to ensure there is some restful sleep before being summoned by Sienna around midnight." Erin was relieved that she did not have to interrupt her busy schedule, but she was also nervous about someone invading her mind while she was sleeping.

Erin hesitated and asked, "Um...when will this training start?"

Anna softly added in a reassuring tone, "Your training will begin Sunday night. It should have started already, but I asked that it be delayed until we had a chance to discuss what was happening first. Try to get some rest this weekend, and Sienna will summon you on Sunday night."

Anna paused and looked sympathetically into Erin's eyes. "I know all of this new information can be very overwhelming. Take some time to digest what I told you, and if you want to talk about it further, just call me."

Erin happily accepted the offer and the chance to take a break from this whole crazy reality for a while. Erin drove back home in a daze. This whole experience was unbelievable, yet after what she had learned from her dad, it was hard to deny it wasn't happening. Thousands of questions were running through her head regarding this whole dream-travel experience.

Thankfully, Dante and Sandra returned soon after Erin got home, and they distracted her with details about which stores they had visited and what they had bought in the mall. Dante noticed Erin's state of mind and offered to pick up take-out dinner from the local Italian restaurant, Nicola's. Erin smiled and agreed right away. They followed their normal Friday routine of an early dinner followed by watching a movie together as a family.

Sandra used to get excited about the prospect of using the air popper. She had a habit of making way too much popcorn, dribbling it liberally with melted butter, and proudly presenting them with three huge bowls of popcorn to enjoy during the movie. Like most activities she used to enjoy, this had become something Sandra no longer wanted to participate in, and Erin resorted to popping a bag of microwave popcorn and watching Sandra text on her cell phone during the whole movie. Erin shrugged it off and figured they were lucky to spend time with Sandra on a Friday night. Her friends were away for the Thanksgiving weekend, or she would most likely have been hanging out with them.

As Erin got ready to go to bed, she felt nervous about the prospect of being summoned during her sleep on Sunday night, but she also felt like she was betraying Dante by not telling him what was going on. She probably should have explained everything to Dante already, but she still didn't understand what was happening herself. Erin justified her silence by deciding that she loved Dante too much to burden him with this issue before she knew all the details herself. The weekend flew by quickly, filled with the usual types of chores and errands.

6

Before Erin knew it, it was Sunday evening, and she was picking out her most conservative flannel pajamas and crawling into bed ahead of schedule at half past nine. Dante was not in bed yet, but she knew he would think she was overtired and be careful not to wake her up. She pushed earplugs into her ears, put her eye mask on, and lay on her back with the blanket tucked around her. Erin tried to relax, but she could not slow her mind. She thought about how she needed to organize the pantry and how she really should rearrange her closet and put away her summer clothes.

Minutes or hours later, she had no idea which, Erin lay thinking about what she should wear to work the next day and wondering if Sandra was going to argue about going to school as she usually did on Monday mornings. A second later, Erin was walking down the stairs of her childhood home. She could see the typical 1970s brown carpeting with orange specs that ran down the middle of the wooden staircase.

As Erin took a step down, her foot slipped off the edge of the step. She threw up her hands to grasp something to catch her balance and only found air. Erin squeezed her eyes shut as she plunged downward, out of control. She landed in a sitting position, and with a start, she registered that it was not the hard landing she had expected. She had crashed onto a soft, moist, bouncy floor.

Erin had experienced similar dreams many times before, but she had always woken up with a start when she fell and then realized she was in her own bed. As Erin opened her eyes this time, she saw that she was definitely not in her own bed. In fact, she was sitting on a moss-covered forest floor. Soft, knee-high green ferns and tropical-looking plants surrounded her. As she stood up and dusted her legs off, she looked upward and saw trees that rose up so high that they appeared to touch the sky. Erin paused when she noticed everything was crystal clear, just like it had been during the dream about her dad. She realized she was dream traveling.

Erin examined her surroundings more closely and saw gigantic trees with huge leaves. Thick, luscious ferns and bushes were covered with exotic-looking flowers. Erin had never visited the Amazon, but she was wondering if that was where she was until she smelled seawater on the warm breeze and realized that she must be on a tropical island. Erin stood a few feet from where she had landed and heard a unique chorus of chirping and clicking bird noises that she had never heard in New Jersey.

As Erin examined her beautiful surroundings, she saw a clearing about twenty feet away and instinctively walked toward it, somehow knowing that was where she was supposed to go. The sense of urgency was slightly unsettling, but it was also comforting to know that she was going in the right direction. Erin was wearing the black pants and lavender blouse she had imagined she would wear to work the next day. As Erin moved forward, she realized it was extremely hot, and she began to sweat in her heavy clothes.

At the opening of the clearing, Erin saw a beautiful mansion that looked like it was almost levitating fifty feet above ground. She approached and saw a breathtaking white staircase gently curving up to the house. Each step of the staircase appeared to be a carved two-foot section of a white tree trunk, and the steps were bound together with some type of embellished metal. Erin could never have imagined that someone could craft a tree trunk into such a sophisticated-looking staircase, yet this staircase looked amazingly elegant and tropical at the same time. She happily started climbing. As she ascended the staircase, she noticed that there was a water system that lightly sprayed her with a soft mist of water as she climbed. Erin found the mist extremely refreshing in the hot climate.

Erin was reminded of the joyful feeling she had as a child when she discovered a hidden room, fort, or tree house. There had been an alluring appeal to hiding in a tree house or fort that made Erin feel like she was in a secret world. For the first time in over twenty years, Erin experienced that joyful feeling as she climbed the tall staircase. As she enjoyed her childish happiness and rounded the top stair, she caught her first up-close glimpse of the perfect dream house to the left of the staircase. The beautiful white mansion had a gorgeous garden in the front that was blooming with flowers in every color, and there was a luxurious pool in the back.

Erin decided that the breathtaking view of the ocean was even better than the mansion and its gardens. The house appeared to be resting on a rock platform that had been carved out of the mountain behind it. From the field below, she had only been able to see the surrounding forest, but from this level she could see above the treetops to the pristine view of the ocean. The water was a gorgeous light-blue color, and gentle waves lapped the beach in the distance. Erin didn't think she could ever get tired of this view.

Erin turned back toward the house, and a pretty young woman in her midtwenties beckoned her over to the garden where she was waiting. She was a little taller than Erin and had long, straight black hair that hung almost to her waist. Her eyes were deep brown and almond-shaped, and she was thin, but with the voluptuous curves of a lingerie model. She was dressed in a simple white sundress that flattered her curves but looked comfortable at the same time.

The stranger offered her right hand and said, "Hello, Erin. I'm Sienna."

Erin relaxed as she realized that she had been summoned to this beautiful place by the Garan, Sienna, and that she had been afraid for no reason—if her wonderful experience so far was any indication.

Erin greeted Sienna, and they settled into soft, cushy outdoor chairs in the middle of Sienna's garden. Erin felt at ease with Sienna right away. Her mannerisms seemed very familiar to Erin, almost as if she knew Sienna already. Erin was older than Sienna by about a decade, so she had an innate feeling that she must know more than this young person. However, Sienna gave the impression of maturity and sophistication.

There was a laptop connected to a projector resting on a small table in the center of the two chairs and a projector screen set up above five feet away. Sienna proceeded to pull her chair toward the laptop and said, "We have a lot to cover tonight, so we should get started. Please feel free to stop me with any questions. I know Anna and Steve shared some information with you, so I'll make sure you learn everything else you need to know."

Sienna sat down and tapped a button on her laptop. As the projector came to life, the first slide appeared with the title *Dream Travel*. Sienna began, "As you know, you can travel back to the time and place you want to go to by thinking about that place before you go to sleep. Typically, it's easiest to dream travel back along your own experiences and your own family lines—both your mother's and father's family lines. Travel outside your family lines is possible, but it's a little more difficult."

Sienna continued, "It's important to wear the appropriate clothes for that time period. The clothes you wear in dream travel will be the last clothes you thought about before you fell asleep, just like the outfit you're wearing right now. When you come back tomorrow night, feel free to think of something more comfortable for this climate."

Erin mentally noted the new information that the training would take more than one night to complete. Sienna must have read Erin's expression and said, "This intense training usually takes at least a week to complete, and you will need supplemental lessons over the next few months."

Erin nodded in acknowledgment, knowing that she had a lot to learn, and she quickly accepted that everything would not be crammed into one night.

Sienna took a deep breath and progressed to the next slide, *Dream Travelers Council (DTC)*. She said, "I would like to get some of the business items out of the way. As Anna told you, there is a ruling body called the Dream Travelers Council or DTC. Dream travelers have the unique ability to travel to the past, observe, and sometimes—under special circumstances—they may need to interact and affect the past experience. That is why it is extremely important to regulate this process. The DTC operates as our regulatory authority."

Sienna explained that Erin was free to dream travel and observe a period of time, but if she wanted to interact with people from the past, she had to gain approval from the DTC prior to the dream travel. Thus, the DTC had become aware of Erin's dream travel because she had an unauthorized interaction with her dad in 1968.

Sienna said, "We know you had no idea what you were doing in your first dream travel, but, hopefully, now you realize the implications of the changes you can cause by interacting during dream travel."

Sienna did not stop with this mind-blowing information. She said the rules of dream travel precluded Erin from using it to benefit herself and/or her family, either financially or politically. Sienna explained that there was a powerful family in the United States that did not heed this warning. They had acted as rogue dream travelers for the past fifty years. As a result they had experienced great success, and equally, they had experienced great tragedy.

"Dream traveling is a gift that runs in families," Sienna explained, "and this particular family fell into the trap of each family member trying to reverse a past tragedy, but instead, they made it worse for themselves."

Erin completely understood this warning and had no intention of trying to pursue anything political. However, she regretted letting go of the brief fantasy she was holding of possibly giving an earlier version of herself some winning lotto numbers to play.

Sienna progressed to the next slide, *DTC Rules,* and continued, "Our most important rule is confidentiality. We live among others, but we are very different from the rest of the population. Every dream traveler would suffer scrutiny if the public found out about us, so confidentiality is vital to all our lives. You are allowed to share your secret with trustworthy members of your family, but obviously, the same rules of confidentiality apply to them also. I say this as a business fact because there are repercussions to breaking this rule." A slide appeared on the projector screen with the title *Confidentiality Breeches.*

The next slide was a picture of the anatomy of the brain with an arrow pointed to a section of the brain. Sienna continued, "Dream travelers have a small benign growth on their pituitary gland. If you violate the rule of confidentiality, the DTC has a group of surgeons that will remove the growth on the brain that allows you to dream travel. You will never be able to dream travel again."

Sienna paused, and she looked sad as she continued. "There was one severe situation where a DT—a dream traveler—violated the rule of confidentiality, and the DTC had the surgery performed on the violator. Even after his surgery had been performed and he was no longer able to dream travel, he was still trying to blackmail the DTC. He said he would expose the DTC and all the DTs he knew.

"Unfortunately, the DTC had to take the punishment to the highest level, and the man was framed for a crime that put him behind bars for life. It was a difficult decision for the DTC to make, but it had to be done. It is harsh, but the punishment for nonDTs who break the confidentiality rule is typically to frame them with a crime."

Erin digested the information with a nod, but she was not too upset by this story, since she knew that she had no intention of ever breaking the confidentiality code and going public with the dream-traveler secret. She doubted anyone would believe her anyway.

The next slide appeared with only the title *Terrents.* Sienna proceed to the following slide: *"Terrent" = The Latin translation of the word "frighten."* Sienna looked at Erin and said, "I believe Anna spoke to you briefly about Terrents. What do you understand about them?"

Erin hesitated and then replied, "Just that they can hijack your dream travel by touching you and thinking of the time they want to travel to."

Sienna nodded in agreement and said, "That is correct. If a Terrent touches you in the time period you're dream traveling in, he or she can hijack your mind and dream travel you to the time that person wants to go to."

After seeing Erin's frightened expression, Sienna reassuringly added, "You don't have to worry. Just follow the rules of the DTC, and they will keep track of your dream travel and save you if you're hijacked by Terrents during dream travel. Only the rogue dream travelers, the ones who function independently and don't follow the DTC rules, are left to fend for themselves with the Terrents."

Sienna proceeded to the next slide, *Terrent Motives,* and said, "Good. Let's go through why Terrents try to hijack us. Terrents are stationed in their own local time, and if they hijack a DT, they can choose any time between the local time and the time the DT is traveling from in the future. Thus, they can travel ahead to a future date and benefit from bringing back knowledge from the future. For example, if a DT who is sleeping in 1999 travels back to 1950 and is hijacked, the hijacking Terrent from 1950 can select any time between 1950 and 1999 to travel to."

Erin began to realize all the implications of Terrent hijacking as Sienna proceeded to the next slide: *Terrent History.*

"Terrents have been around for thousands of years. They have been traveling forward in time and have been 'inventing' the technology they witnessed from the future. Some of the most famous inventors are Terrents."

Erin could not help thinking about all the past famous inventors and wondering if they were Terrents.

Sienna added, "As communication improved over the past two hundred years, Terrents have united and organized their approach.

Have you noticed how fast technology has progressed over the past two hundred years? The computer chip, the Internet, the stealth bomber…" Sienna paused and smiled when she saw Erin's expression of shock and amazement. Then she continued.

"For thousands of years, technology progressed at a snail's pace, but once the first mail system was in place and communication spread across regions, the Terrents became very powerful. The Terrent organization is called the Tara League. The Tara League is currently so sophisticated and organized that its members probably already know, or will soon know, that you are our newest dream traveler."

Sienna tapped a key on her laptop, and the next slide appeared: *Terrent Damage*. "The Garans and dream travelers understand and respect the intricacies of time travel, and we try not to impact a time that we are visiting. However, the Terrents have no respect for the time continuum and recklessly maneuver when they hijack a dream traveler. They interact with local people and cause major shifts in a time period. Since these moments in time have already occurred, these shifts in time have an impact on the time continuum and, in turn, on the physical environment of the earth. These major shifts destabilize the earth's physical environment and have led to many disasters that have been labeled as natural disasters but were actually due to the destabilization caused by the shift in the time continuum.

"I think the best way to describe this phenomenon is to imagine the brick foundation of a house. If someone removes lower bricks of the foundation and creates a hole, the bricks above the hole will crash down. Thus, if someone was inclined to believe that the recent increase in technological inventions was a positive result of Terrent activity, one would just have to consider the major increase in the number of natural disasters that have occurred as a result of the destabilization that the Terrents have caused to see that the inventions have a terrible cost."

Erin nodded in agreement as she tried to digest all of this new information.

Sienna took a look at her watch and said, "I think we have covered a lot tonight, and we should probably wait until tomorrow night to continue. Do you have any questions?"

Erin had a lot of questions and said, "What happens to my sleeping body while I am dream traveling?"

"Nothing. Your body is sleeping, and if someone or something wakes you, you just exit your dream travel when you wake up."

Erin asked, "Since you summoned me, and it is daylight right now, where are we now, and what day is it?"

Sienna answered, "We are at my house on the island of Dominica, and it is yesterday, Saturday. This is an isolated place where we can complete your training without interacting with anyone else."

Erin then said, "Anna said that dream travel usually starts at puberty; do you know why I have started so late in life?"

Sienna sat back looking surprised and said, "I'm sorry; I thought you already knew. I would have discussed that topic first if I had known. Your pregnancy probably triggered your dream travel. When I summoned you tonight, I felt your energy and a unique, separate energy."

Erin's jaw dropped immediately, and she stuttered, "Preg... pregnancy?"

Sienna replied nervously, "Yes, you didn't know you are pregnant?"

Erin swallowed hard and said, "No, I had no idea." Erin was mentally calculating her last period in her mind and realized that she was probably a week or two late, but her period was sometimes erratic.

Sienna continued, "Well, you obviously had the physical ability to dream travel your whole life, but your puberty hormones did not trigger it, and it has just been triggered due to the hormone spike of your pregnancy."

Erin's mind was racing. She wanted children, but Dante was a little reluctant to have more. They had agreed to postpone the decision about whether to have kids until the summer, and they were being careful to prevent pregnancy. Thus, Erin was in shock that she was pregnant.

Sienna noticed this and looked a little uncomfortable with the whole situation. She turned to Erin and said, "Do you need more time to deal with this? We could postpone the training sessions..."

Erin got a hold of herself and said, "No, it's OK. We should continue on schedule. I am definitely surprised by this, but it's much more important that I am prepared for dream travel."

Sienna looked relieved that Erin had some color back in her face and said, "OK, if that's it, I will send you back and will see you tomorrow night."

Erin nodded and said, "Yes, thank you, Sienna. I know this training must be a nuisance, but I do appreciate it."

Sienna smiled and said, "My pleasure. I am glad we have such a good person joining our ranks." She paused and then said, "If you lie back in that lounge chair and close your eyes, I will send you back to your own bed." They said good-bye, and Erin did as Sienna instructed, relaxing in the lounge chair and closing her eyes.

7

Light was streaming in around the window shade, and Dante was snoring lightly in her ear. She looked at him sleeping peacefully and felt a wave of compassion. He was going to have a lot to deal with. Her life had changed so much in the past few days that she didn't know how to explain everything. Erin took a deep breath and decided to come up with a plan. First she had to confirm the pregnancy. Then she would talk to Dante and explain how she had found out she was pregnant and explain the whole dream-travel thing. As hard as this was going to be to explain, Erin knew it would probably be harder for poor Dante to believe all of this craziness.

Almost instinctively, Erin's hands slid to her stomach. She imagined the idea of a baby growing inside her, but she couldn't quite believe it yet. It seemed too unreal to be true. Erin actually felt guilty because she was longing for a baby, and it almost seemed unfair to Dante, who was not ready to have another child. She didn't have confirmation, and she needed that medical confirmation to really start believing that she was pregnant.

Erin glanced at the alarm clock and saw that it was six o'clock. She grudgingly left the bed to get an early start with a shower. She knew her gynecologist office opened at eight o'clock, and there was a chance she might be able to get an emergency appointment set up for today if she started calling as soon as they opened.

Luck was on Erin's side because, thanks to a cancelation, she was able to squeeze into an appointment with her gynecologist, Dr. Ruben, at half past one that afternoon. She felt guilty about running to the doctor's office during work hours, so she worked extra hard through the morning and ate her sandwich at her desk.

Erin arrived at Dr. Ruben's office promptly at 1:29 p.m. and sat nervously for ten minutes before she was called by the office nurse, Theresa, to provide a urine sample. Erin had met Theresa on previous checkup visits and really liked her sweet, easygoing nature. Theresa was in her late thirties and wore a short bob of tight, light-brown curls. Erin had noticed and appreciated that Theresa always went out of her way to make her patients feel comfortable.

The urine sample was a standard part of every gynecologist office visit, but this time Erin felt differently about providing the urine sample. For the first time in her life, this sample might be positive. As Erin handed over her sample, she suddenly felt insecure about not doing a home pregnancy test before this visit. She had told the office manager that she thought she was pregnant and needed an appointment urgently, and the office manager had just assumed that she had a positive home pregnancy test.

Erin was hit with a new wave of fear because she had begged the office staff to fit her in. What if she was just going crazy, and these dreams were the first symptoms of her psychosis? Erin quietly cursed herself for not thinking this whole thing through more carefully. As Erin waited for Dr. Ruben in the examination room, she wondered if this whole visit was just a false alarm. Although she worried that the staff would be annoyed, her doubt actually made Erin feel better. If the test was negative, she would be able to confirm that both the dream travel and the pregnancy idea were figments of her imagination, and her life would go back to normal.

Dr. Ruben knocked on the examination room door and came in with Theresa. Dr. Ruben was a slender man in his midforties, with soft brown eyes that exuded concern. From the look of his thinning hair and the worry lines on his forehead, Erin could tell that he was protective and cared for all his patients as if they were part of his family. He had obviously earned the multiple awards hanging on the walls of his office that indicated he was one of the top OB-GYN doctors in the state of New Jersey.

"Hello, Erin, how are you feeling?" asked Dr. Ruben.

"I am fine and you?" Erin responded.

Dr. Ruben answered, "Very well, thank you. Well, congratulations! Just as you thought, your urine test here confirmed that you're pregnant. Do you know when the first day of your last cycle was?"

Erin hesitated and then slowly answered, "I think it was around October tenth."

Dr. Ruben said, "That's good because it's very early in your pregnancy, but we need to a do a few things right away. First, I need you to start taking prenatal vitamins right away. I will be doing some blood tests today to screen for genetic diseases. I also suggest that you start taking additional folic acid and calcium supplements. Of course we will need to get you scheduled for follow-up visits and ultrasounds, but Theresa will set those up with you."

Dr. Ruben briefly examined her as he gave advice and instructions. As the doctor spoke and examined Erin, her head was spinning… Sienna was right! More important, this was another confirmation that dream travel was real and she was not going crazy.

As Dr. Ruben washed and dried his hands, he noticed Erin's expression and asked, "Erin, are you OK? I know this is a big adjustment. So if you want to go home, digest this information, talk to your husband, and call me with any questions, that would be fine, too."

Erin pulled herself together, smiled, and said, "Yes, that would be good."

Dr. Ruben punched a few keys on his laptop and said, "From my calculations your due date is July seventeenth. Have you had any nausea or cramping?"

Erin thought about it and responded, "Well, about a week ago, I had some menstrual cramps but no bleeding. I haven't felt nauseous or vomited, but my mom and sister never had morning sickness, so hopefully I will be the same."

Dr. Ruben said, "All right, please give the office a call to let me know if you do have any spotting or excessive vomiting."

Erin nodded in agreement.

Dr. Ruben smiled and said, "OK, look at your calendar and give Theresa a call to set up those appointments and please feel free to call me anytime with any questions you may have. I will see you in about a week for your first ultrasound."

Erin left the doctor's office with a Band-Aid on her arm from the blood draw, a bag full of prenatal vitamin samples, and a prescription for folic acid supplements. She was in a daze as she drove back to work. Erin could really use a nice, big glass of wine on a day like this, but that wouldn't be an option for her for a long time. She was going to have to figure out a way to break this news to Dante after she got home.

She made it through the rest of the workday and the evening completely distracted, and she went through the routine motions of picking Sandra up, making dinner, and cleaning up the kitchen without much talking. Erin was only delaying the inevitable, but when she found out that Dante was on call and would not be home until after ten o'clock, she decided that the news could wait until tomorrow.

Erin started winding down to go to bed at nine o'clock, and as she was setting her alarm clock, she noticed an old clothes catalog on her bedside table. It was from at least six months ago, but as she glanced at it, she saw a page that she had flagged with a sticky note. When she flipped to the page, she saw the picture of a long, flowing blue sundress she had been thinking about ordering last June. For the first time all day, Erin felt a little playful and wondered if it would really work. She imagined the sundress as she lay back in bed and closed her eyes.

8

Erin didn't remember falling asleep, but when she stood up in the clearing, she saw that it was a beautiful, sunny day in Dominica. She walked over to the bottom of Sienna's white staircase and noticed that she was wearing the blue sundress from the catalog. As she climbed the staircase and admired the sundress, Erin decided there were some nice perks to being a dream traveler. Sienna greeted her with a hug at the top of the stairs, and they walked over to the chairs and the projector in the garden.

Sienna asked, "I can just imagine that your day was crazy with all you learned last night; are you doing OK?"

Erin said, "Yes, I saw my doctor, and he confirmed that I'm pregnant and that everything is fine so far." Erin paused before continuing. "I know you summoned me here, but is it OK to dream travel while I'm pregnant?"

Sienna nodded as she answered, "As far as we know, there should be no negative effects of dream travel on your unborn baby."

Erin looked relieved. "My last gigantic hurdle will be explaining a pregnancy and dream travel to my husband."

Sienna looked sympathetic and said, "Let me know how it works out. It's always hard to get a spouse to understand dream travel, but we can always help you if we have to."

Erin couldn't think of how Sienna could help, but she thanked her anyway.

"I hope you don't mind, but we have a lot to cover, so we will get started right away."

Erin nodded in agreement as Sienna started the projector, and the first slide appeared. The slide said, *Preventing Terrent Travel.* Sienna began the training session by saying, "Anna might have told you that all human beings hear a mild ringing in their ears when a DT is present within a close area. This ringing is different for Terrents. Terrents hear the ringing when a DT is within a hundred yards, and the ringing becomes more pronounced as they get closer. Thus, once Terrents know what they can do with their gift, it's easy to find a DT by just listening and following the ringing in their ears. The ringing sound is so alluring to a Terrent that it's hard to think of anything else besides finding the source of the sound."

Sienna continued, "Terrents are different than dream travelers because there is no anatomical part of the brain that can be altered to prevent them from hijacking dream travelers. However, about seventy-five years ago, we discovered that fluoride interferes with their ability to hijack DTs. Thus, the Dream Traveler Council is a strong supporter of fluoridated water, toothpaste with fluoride, and enriching children's vitamins with fluoride."

Erin thought about her own fluoridated toothpaste and how most dental hygiene products included fluoride. She was amazed that something so common in her life tied back to the influence of the DTC. Sienna saw Erin's surprised expression and said, "Don't get me wrong; of course fluoride is good for dental health. However, the DTC has taken advantage of that fact to prevent Terrent hijackings, and the long-term impact has been beneficial for society with better overall dental health. It is sort of a win-win situation."

Erin had no complaints about a group that controlled the enemy by a simple supplement that improved all of society's overall dental health. She nodded in agreement and said, "Wow, if only all of the world's problems could be solved that way."

Sienna smiled and said, "Unfortunately, the Terrents have caught on, and most of them avoid fluoride products at all cost. Most active Terrents shun fluoridated toothpaste and vitamins, and as a result many Terrents have horrible teeth. However, the DTC hasn't given up. Recently, we have genetically altered some grains grown in the United States so that they contain small amounts of fluoride. Since the United States is a major exporter of wheat and grains to the rest of the world, this has had a global impact. We are also working on secretely genetically altering the other grain and rice producers of the world."

Erin was amazed with the DTC's foresight, and with a new pride, she said, "That is a great idea."

Sienna hesitated and said, "Well, the DTC thought so, too, but Terrents have an amazing communication network, and the ones who know about the genetically altered grains have already taken up gluten-free diets."

Erin sighed and said, "That stinks."

Sienna looked a little defeated but added, "I know, but the DTC will never stop looking for new ways to interrupt the Terrents' ability to hijack DTs." Sienna paused and said, "The one topic we haven't really talked about is obviously something I am very familiar with, Garans." Sienna flipped to the next slide, titled *Garans*. "Garans are identifiable because they are born with a triangular birthmark on the palm of one of their hands or on one of the soles of their feet."

As Sienna said this, she turned her left hand palm up and showed Erin something that she hadn't noticed before. In the middle of Sienna's left palm, there was a light-brown, triangular birthmark about the size of a dime. Erin noticed that the triangle was only a shade or two darker than the surrounding skin.

Erin stared as she realized that she had never seen a birthmark on someone's palms or on the soles of the feet. Sienna continued, "Garans are similar to dream travelers in how they start dream traveling at puberty. They can be summoned like other dream travelers. However, there is no surgical or chemical way to stop a Garan from dream traveling, so they are considered the most powerful dream travelers."

Sienna proceeded to the next slide and said, "In addition to dream traveling in the past, we have the ability to dream travel forward into the future. Due to the implications of future travel, it's never done without full DTC consideration and approval. Future travel is considered sacred and is only considered under special circumstances."

Erin was trying to remain casual and cool about everything she was learning, but it was hard to hide her curiosity, and she blurted out, "Have you dream traveled into the future?"

Sienna responded, "Yes, several times for DTC business."

Erin felt she had been a little rude and chose not to pursue the subject.

Sienna proceeded to the next slide: *Garan Summoning Role* and paused for a moment. "Obviously, I have been summoning you here to Dominica, and I hope you can forgive me for the next piece of information I will share with you."

Erin was puzzled and tried to arrange her face in an understanding expression. She already liked Sienna and could not fathom why she would ask for forgiveness.

Sienna softened her expression and said, "In order for me to be able to summon you, I had to violate your privacy and place a summoning sachet under the mattress of your bed. I dream traveled to your bedroom the day you met with Anna, when no one was home, and placed the sachet and left. I was only in your home for about a minute, and I tried not to disturb anything. Again, I sincerely apologize for violating your privacy."

Erin was not upset by this minor fact, and she smiled. "That's fine, but what is a summoning sachet?"

Sienna's tense questioning eyebrows relaxed and smoothed out, and she smiled and said, "There are personal items from each of the six Garans in the sachet. Garans can only summon dream travelers by placing a summoning sachet under the dreamer's bed or near the area where he or she is sleeping. If possible, please remember to take the sachet with you when you travel or spend the night away. After your training is completed, you will only be summoned if there is a DTC meeting or an urgent issue.

"Obviously, you have already experienced the pull from your own dream that creates a falling or pulling sensation when you are summoned."

Erin smiled and nodded knowingly. Erin thought it was strange that she had been sleeping over a summoning sachet for the past few days, and she made a mental note to check her bed when she woke up. At the same moment, Erin saw a movement out of the corner of her eye and turned her head to get a better look.

Her shock must have been apparent because Sienna quickly touched Erin's arm with a comforting pat and said, "It's OK. Remember the sleeping versions of ourselves are in current time, and I dream traveled back in time and then summoned you. Thus, we are dream traveling back in time to my home right now, so the awake version of me from yesterday is walking around."

Erin was speechless and sat with her mouth open slightly, as she watched an identical-twin version of Sienna walking past the front of the house. The awake version of Sienna was walking and carrying a basket. She noticed Erin staring and gave a gentle wave before walking over to a vegetable garden and starting to pick grapes from a vine that covered the back wall of the property.

Erin hesitated and then said, "Is that weird for you?"

Sienna smiled and said, "I have been training new dream travelers for years here at my home, so it's very normal for me to see my awake self when I am dream traveling and my dream traveling self when I am awake."

"Wow, I am sorry for acting so surprised, but I hadn't even thought of that yet," said Erin.

Sienna said, "I have seen others react badly when this has happened in the past. I am glad it didn't disturb you too much."

Erin shook her head and said, "There are so many implications to think about."

Sienna nodded. She started shutting down her laptop and said, "We should probably let you get back to sleep and pick up here tomorrow night."

Erin agreed and hugged Sienna. She knew the routine of what to do next. Erin lay back in the lounge chair and closed her eyes. Just as on the previous night, the next thing she knew, she was back in her own bed next to Dante.

9

The alarm went off at a quarter past six, and Erin opened one eye to watch Dante roll over, climb out of bed, and walk toward the bathroom to take a shower. With this new schedule of working all day and DT training all night, Erin felt like she was definitely falling behind on true rest. It was like her mind was active twenty-four hours a day, and she wondered if this lack of rest for her mind would hurt her after a while. Her thoughts were interrupted by the sound of the water in the shower, and she knew it was time to start her day and go and grab some coffee for Dante and herself.

As Erin filled the two cups with coffee and added creamer, she contemplated whether this morning was a good time to tell Dante what was going on. He definitely deserved to know. Erin was so preoccupied lately that Dante might already be wondering what was distracting her. She decided it was time to tell him. As she climbed the stairs with the coffee, she noticed that there was no light or noise coming from Sandra's room, which could only mean that she had overslept. Erin took a detour and tapped lightly on Sandra's door.

As soon as she opened the door, she heard Sandra straining her voice to say, "I am not going to school. I don't feel good."

Erin could tell that Sandra was faking illness and was not even going to try to cajole her to get up. Erin turned and walked down the hall to the bathroom to greet Dante with the news of Sandra's declaration.

Dante rolled his eyes as soon as Erin gave him the update and said, "She needs to grow up and realize that we all have to get up in the morning, and maybe if she didn't spend so much time on the computer at nighttime, it would be easier to wake up!"

Dante put on his robe and stormed out of the bathroom, down the hallway, and into Sandra's room. From the bathroom Erin could hear the argument that ensued. By the time Erin was finished showering, she heard Sandra moving around getting ready to go to school, and she saw Dante walking around in a foul mood. Erin gave him a warm hug and tried to cheer him up as he picked up his keys and cell phone. It worked slightly, but there was no hope of breaking the news to him this morning. It was Dante's morning to drop Sandra off at school, so they all said good-bye in the garage and went their separate ways.

Erin had a teleconference at half past seven with the physicians on the scientific-advisory board who were responsible for reviewing the data from the pancreatic cancer study she was working on. They met every two weeks with the global-study team partners around the world, and this scientific-advisory board to discuss the quality of the data that was being received. Thankfully, Erin was able to attend this meeting via teleconference and did not have to be present in the office for each meeting. She turned the car radio off and listened via her cell phone as she drove to work.

The teleconference went smoothly, except for one minor, heated discussion between Molly and Dr. Lang. Erin signed off the call just as she entered the front door of her office building. As she walked over to her desk, she saw Molly sitting in front of her computer with a red face, red ears, and pale circles around her eyes. Erin knew that although Molly was young, her blood pressure went up when she was very upset, and then she had a typical "hypertension face."

When Molly saw Erin, she said, "Stop laughing at me!"

Erin felt a flash of guilt, and then she smiled and said, "I'm not laughing at you; I just think it's cute that you get so passionate about this."

Molly assumed a pouting face, and then she exploded. "I just think that it is so unfair how Dr. Lang always picks on the study sites that I manage. Why does he always do that? It's ridiculous how he attacks my sites and no one else's!"

Erin calmly said, "Relax. Dr. Lang has low self-esteem and is just trying to get a rise out of you. You can't let this get to you. Life is too short."

Erin knew that Molly had the same type of work ethic that she did and that Molly took the criticism from Dr. Lang personally, but Erin also knew that Molly needed to get a thicker skin. She didn't want to see her friend make herself sick over work issues. When Molly kept her pouty face and shrugged, Erin decided to distract her and asked, "Do you want to go for coffee?"

Molly looked down at her empty coffee cup and quickly agreed. Erin spent the trip to the cafeteria distracting Molly with a funny story about how Dante had teased her two months ago, the first time she had to have a mammography, by texting her saying he wanted pancakes for dinner. Erin explained that she had been ready to pick up pancake mix until she realized that Dante was teasing about what the mammography machine was going to do her chest. Molly's laugh burst out, and she continued laughing until her eyes filled with tears. By the time they got back from coffee, Molly's face was back to normal, and she was ready to get to work.

Erin asked, "Do you want to go to that Greek restaurant you like for lunch today?" Erin knew that Molly loved Greek food and thought that would definitely get her mind off Dr. Lang.

Molly smiled and said, "Yes, wait…oh, no, I have to go to the dentist for a filling today. How about tomorrow?"

Erin nodded in agreement and said, "Absolutely; tomorrow will be perfect."

It was funny to Erin how close she had grown to her friends at work. When they were upset, she was actually unable to work well. She had worked at several different places prior to this job, but she had never felt closer to her coworkers than she did at Kaso Pharmaceuticals. It was actually nice to go to go in every day and know that other people cared about her so much that they felt like an extended family. In turn she usually wound up telling them almost everything about her personal life and relied on their advice to help guide her. Part of Erin felt sad that she couldn't share the dream-traveler information with them and, especially, that she couldn't speak to Molly about it. Erin was having information overload about the dream-traveler stuff, and she thought it would be so nice to be able to talk about it with someone.

As Erin thought about her need to tell someone about what was happening, she realized that she was allowed to share the information with Dante and that he definitely was overdue to hear it anyway. Erin plugged through the rest of the day at work, using every free minute to plan the best way to break the news to Dante. In the end she decided that Dante was a man of science and that factual information was the best approach to explaining dream travel and the pregnancy. Erin was not that religious, but she said a few extra prayers that day that everything would be OK when she broke the news.

All went smoothly during the normal routine of picking Sandra up from school, stopping at the grocery store for dinner, and making, eating, and cleaning up dinner. Once dinner was over, Erin watched Dante's movements like a hawk, waiting and counting down the minutes until he started getting ready to go to bed. She carefully thought about everything she was going to say once they were alone in their bedroom.

Erin heard Dante sit on the bed as she was brushing her teeth. She spent the last minute in the bathroom trying to calm the butterflies in her stomach. She slowly made her way to the bedroom and crawled into bed with Dante, who was already lying down. Erin sat back against the pillows, pulled the blankets up, and turned to face her husband.

"Can we talk about something?" she asked.

Dante's face took on the look of dread that men often get when they hear their wife ask that question, and he nodded.

Erin felt guilty just from the look on his face. She took a deep breath and started, "You didn't do anything wrong. I just have two things to tell you that are very bizarre, but you need to know these things right away."

At that point they both took a deep breath. Erin cautiously continued. "This is going to sound insane, but I just found out that I am a dream traveler, and I have the ability to travel back in time when I am sleeping. There are others like me, and all of us dream travelers have a growth on our pituatary gland that allows us to do this. Most dream travelers start being able to dream travel when their hormones increase during puberty, but that didn't happen to me."

Erin noted that Dante's eyes were wide open and his facial features were relaxed in a calm expression as he asked in a curious voice, "You can travel back in time?"

Erin responded, "Yes."

Dante nodded his head and seemed like he accepted this completely ridiculous fact. "OK," he replied.

This positive response made Erin feel so much better that it gave her the confidence to approach the much more typical fact with confidence. She said, "My dream-traveler ability stayed dormant in puberty, but it just activated because my hormones started to change. Dante, the next thing I have to tell you is that I went to Dr. Ruben, and he confirmed that I am pregnant."

Erin's confidence was shattered in the second it took for Dante to absorb that fact because his expression and his body language changed completely. His pleasant, open expression quickly turned to disappointment, and he went from sitting up in bed to slumping forward in a defeated posture.

Erin was so surprised and hurt by this response that she could barely talk. Dante filled in the silence with a long sigh. Erin choked back the tears that had welled up in her eyes and said, "Why are you so upset?"

Dante only looked more injured by her question. "I am upset because I thought we were waiting to decide whether to have children."

Erin was aghast at what he was insinuating. "Do you think this is my fault? We have purposely been careful, and this just happened. You're looking at me like it's my fault!" Erin's hurt quickly turned to anger, and she said, "The worst part is that I told you something completely out of this world, that I am a dream traveler, and you were OK with that, but when I tell you about something completely normal—especially for a couple in love—you look like I stabbed you in the heart!"

Erin was reeling from his obvious revulsion. She couldn't help feeling a horrible heartache because he rejected the idea of having a child with her and looked as if it were the end of the world.

Erin had spent her whole life looking forward to the day that she would be able to have her own child. However, she had purposely taken every precaution to make sure that she didn't have a child before she was financially and emotionally ready for it. Erin had sacrificed for years to make the right career moves to ensure she would make a good salary for the rest of her life.

Dante had known from the moment that they had started dating that Erin definitely wanted children. She was an honest person and felt it would be unfair to hide that truth from him, and she had been up-front all along. The irony was that they were currently being careful about their family planning.

Erin didn't think she was beautiful, but from Dante's expression of distaste, it seemed he thought he would be having a child with the worst person in the world! She was so hurt that she could barely speak, and when she was able to get the words out, she said with tears streaming down her face, "Am I so bad that you're horrified about having a baby with me?"

That comment hit Dante like a bomb, and he realized what he had done. He gulped and said, "I never meant it to come across like that! I am upset because, financially, we're not ready to have a child. The alimony I am paying to my ex is killing me. Sandra is living with us full time, and I'm paying for all her expenses, but most of my salary is still going to Susan.

"As you know, when I got divorced, I gave her the house so that Sandra could continue to live in the house where she had grown up. I also agreed to sign over most of my salary in alimony payments to make sure Sandra was comfortable. Obviously, when my ex started dating Harry, Sandra was unhappy and came to live with us full time, but the financial terms of my divorce have not changed.

"To make matters worse, the Medicare reimbursement for doctors has dropped significantly, and I am working harder than ever but getting paid less. It took me four years of medical school and six years of training to be able to perform a bronchoscopy*, and we just paid the plumber more money for the time he spent fixing our kitchen sink than I get reimbursed from Medicare to perform one!"

Dante took a deep breath and put his arms around Erin. Erin was a little resistant, but Dante rubbed her back and after a few minutes, she relaxed.

Dante continued, "I didn't mean to come across like I was rejecting you. I'm just really worried about our financial future."

Erin was still sobbing and said, "It isn't fair, though. I make a good salary, but because of your past, I am suffering and have to be upset about having a baby, when I should be excited! I feel like I worked too hard to have to think like this! I am thirty-five, and most of my friends have multiple children and have been able to enjoy being a mother. Meanwhile, I have waited to have children to get ahead in my career and to become financially stable, but now I have to suffer because of your past!"

Dante nodded in surrender and said, "You're right. I'm sorry I said all of that. I was taken by surprise and had a knee-jerk reaction.

We'll figure out how we will do this financially, and everything will work out."

Erin took a deep breath and relaxed in his arms. He was still rubbing her back, and Erin was starting to feel a wave of relief that she had shared everything with Dante. It felt like a ton of bricks were lifted off her shoulders.

Dante must have sensed she was relaxing and lightened the mood by cracking a joke: "You know there are some good things about this pregnancy. Your boobs are going to be huge!"

Erin laughed until she cried tears of happiness; they were a team again. They were going to handle all of this craziness together, and they were going to survive.

They curled up in each other's arms and eventually drifted to their normal sleeping positions. Every couple has a favorite way of sleeping, and Erin thought of their usual position as the "heart." They both slept on their backs holding hands. Erin's left hand held Dante's right, and her left foot touched Dante's right foot, making a perfect heart shape. Erin was aware that the idea was dorky, but she loved how it felt to fall asleep connected to Dante.

10

E rin was so exhausted that she barely remembered falling, but the next thing she knew, she felt the soft bump of grass under her feet, and she was standing in the clearing in Dominica. The last outfit she must have thought of was the pajamas she wore to bed because she noticed she was wearing them as she rounded the top step and saw Sienna waving her over to the garden. She walked over happily, and Sienna greeted her with a warm hug. Erin thought about how quickly she had become attached to Sienna. It almost felt like Sienna was a sister or a best friend. Erin was relieved to tell Sienna how things had gone with Dante. Erin quickly unloaded all the details and sat back to hear Sienna's response. Sienna seemed a little taken aback that Dante had accepted the dream-traveler information so easily.

Sienna raised her eyebrows and said, "I understand his hesitation with accepting the pregnancy, but I am surprised that he was really OK with the whole dream-traveler thing."

Erin was exhausted from the whole experience and just could not put any more energy into questioning Dante's response, so she just shook her head in acknowledgment. Erin said, "Dante has teased me in the past, saying I am a witch, when I have guessed what is going to happen or have predicted what a person's real motives were and my predictions came true. I think he has always suspected that I was a little different from everyone else. Maybe that's why he was so accepting of the dream-traveler update?"

Sienna still hesitated, but she finally nodded her head in agreement.

Erin could tell that she was concerned about Dante's ready acceptance of dream travel. She pushed it out of her mind and asked, "Do we have a lot to cover tonight?"

Sienna took that as her cue to get started, opened the slide presentation to a slide with the title *How to Dream Travel*, and said, "Yes, the first thing we are going to cover is something you will be doing very soon. As a dream traveler, all you have to do is to concentrate on the date in the past that you want to visit before you fall asleep at night, and you should be able to dream travel yourself there. You have to be extremely careful in every interaction you have with another human on these experiences, because any type of interaction could cause massive changes in that time."

Erin nodded in acknowledgment as she thought about the time she had dream traveled back to 1968. Erin realized that she must have been thinking about her father and 1968 the night before she fell asleep.

Sienna noticed that Erin was deep in thought and brought her back to the moment by saying, "I am guessing you are trying to remember your dream-travel experience. However, I need your complete attention for tonight's training session."

Erin snapped back to the moment, repositioned herself in her chair, and gave Sienna her full attention.

Sienna said, "You also saw that I was OK with allowing the physical version of myself to see my dream-traveling self the other night because the physical version is aware of my ability. This same rule applies to you. The only physical versions of 'Erin' that can be allowed to see you during dream travel would be from this point in time forward. You are not allowed to let yourself be visible to the earlier versions of yourself who did not know about your dream-traveling ability."

Erin nodded in agreement and thought of how frightening it would have been to see a clone of herself before she knew about dream travel.

Sienna continued, "The most important thing you can do when you dream travel is blend into the background of the time and place you're visiting so no one notices you. Be aware of the style at the time and pick conservative outfits that blend easily. I typically image a very plain outfit and often choose to wear a baseball cap pulled down to hide my face or plain sunglasses during the daytime to further disguise myself.

"Then I think of precisely where I want to appear and exactly when. Sometimes, it's hard to pick an exact time, so I typically think of the segment of the day, such as morning, afternoon, evening, or night. Once I have thought all of that through, I think of where I could appear that would not attract attention and what activity I could do to immediately blend in. It is so important that you do not interact in any way. Obviously, this means not talking to anyone, but even something as innocent as accidentally bumping into someone can affect the time continuum."

Erin was fairly insightful, and her brain immediately went into overload thinking about the infinite number of implications of accidentally affecting a time period she was only meant to observe. She had a new appreciation for the complexity of dream travel, and she began to feel more apprehensive about her future dream travel.

As if Sienna sensed this, she said, "I think it is time that you actually try out dream travel for yourself tomorrow night. In fact, tomorrow night I want you to dream travel on your own, and the following night we can meet and review everything you felt and did in your dream travel."

Erin gulped and said, "Are you sure I'm ready?"

Sienna smiled and said, "I think we have reviewed a lot of information over the past few days, and it's time to work on your practical skills. Take a minute right now and think of a happy time that you would not mind going back to and observing."

Erin concentrated, and the first thing that came to mind was her first kiss with Dante. She thought about how magical that moment was and how much it had changed her life.

Erin realized that she would never be a good poker player, because Sienna let out a laugh and said, "This must be a great memory because you are blushing!"

Erin smiled with amusement and said, "Yes, I was actually thinking of my first kiss with my husband. Without giving away too many gooey details, it was one of those magical moments in my life that I wouldn't mind going back and observing."

Sienna smiled a knowing smile and said, "That's perfect. Now I need you to do some homework. I know that was not too long ago, but I want you to look up the things that were in style about six months before that time, and pick the most conservative outfit you can. Obviously, you should also pick something like a hat or sunglasses to disguise yourself even further.

"Tonight when you go to bed, think of the exact date, time, and place that you want to be, and think about the outfit you should be wearing. You should make sure you are a little distance from where the kiss happened. You also might want to make sure you think of a hidden place where people don't usually go, so that your sudden appearance doesn't stand out."

Sienna continued, "Once you fall asleep, your mind will do the rest. Sometimes DTs have a typical door that they travel through. I have been summoning you here for the past few days, but the day of your first dream-travel experience, when you saw your father, was there a door involved?"

Erin answered, "Yes, it was actually the door in the sanitation garage where my father used to work."

Sienna nodded and said, "OK, there is a chance that it will be the same tonight when you dream travel; however, it may be a different door. The most important thing is that you not be distracted and forget all the rules we discussed."

Erin nodded and looked at Sienna, nervous but excited, and said, "I think I'm ready, but after all of those warnings, I'm nervous that I will mess up."

Sienna gave Erin an encouraging smile. "Remember, if you focus on blending into the background, you'll blend in without a problem. I'm sure you'll do great."

Erin took a deep breath and nodded in agreement.

Sienna said, "I am going to let you get a little more rest tonight. Tomorrow night, dream travel and observe as we discussed. You should be able to observe the time period you would like and wake up a short time after."

Erin said, "OK, thank you, Sienna." She gave Sienna a hug and followed the routine of lying down in the lounge chair and closing her eyes.

11

The next thing Erin remembered was hearing the alarm at half past six. Her morning started like every other, but this time she was excited, yet nervous, about her upcoming dream travel. Erin ate her breakfast bar and took one of her new prenatal vitamins, along with a calcium and vitamin D tablet, before she left the house. She had been summoned to dream travel every night for the past few days, but that was easy because it was so passive. Tonight she would have to dream travel on her own and follow all the DT rules flawlessly. In theory it sounded like an easy task, but Erin liked to succeed in everything she did, and she was nervous that she was going to let Sienna down or, even worse, somehow mess up the time continuum by accident.

Erin drove to work in a haze and went through her day totally distracted. It was so hard to believe that she had a gift that allowed her to time travel and that tonight she would go back and physically observe the moment that she had tried to relive a million times in her mind. Her first kiss with Dante had truly been a turning point in her relationship with him, and she was a little nervous that maybe she had misinterpreted it or remembered it out of proportion. Erin tried to push all of those thoughts out of her mind so she could focus on work.

It was a long, trying day of meetings and responding to e-mails, but Erin got through it and finally made it home. She was sitting at the table with Dante and Sandra, eating dinner, when she realized that she only had a few hours until she would be officially dream traveling on her own! Dante and Sandra seemed a little apprehensive during dinner, almost as if they sensed her anticipation.

Erin pushed through dinner, quickly cleaned up afterward, and was soon on the Internet, confirming the clothes styles of New Jersey in the fall of the year of her first kiss with Dante. Erin decided that black workout pants with a white stripe down the side and a white T-shirt were very typical of that year. A black baseball cap pulled down to hide most of her face would complete the look, while appearing perfectly normal for a physically active resident of Hoboken, New Jersey, who lived at that time.

Erin started getting ready for bed a little earlier than normal and was in the bathroom brushing her teeth when Dante walked in and closed the bathroom door. Dante looked strained and concerned, and he nervously asked, "Do you feel OK?"

Erin rinsed out and dried her mouth and walked over and put her arms around Dante. She smiled and felt a wave of love for this man who was so concerned for her. She knew that he must have misinterpreted her unusual behavior during dinner as a symptom of something wrong with the pregnancy, and he looked scared.

Erin responded, "Everything is fine. I'm sorry for acting weird during dinner. I think you'll laugh if I tell you why I'm so distracted."

Dante remained quiet and raised his eyebrows in a questioning way.

Erin hesitated and said, "Remember when I said that I was a dream traveler?"

Dante nodded and folded his arms in front of him.

Erin continued, "Well, it sounds crazy, but I have been in training sessions while I sleep for the past few nights, and tonight is the first night that I will select a time and go dream travel on my own."

Dante's expression changed to a look of confusion, and he said, "I don't get it. I know about the pregnancy now, and I have accepted it. There is no need to create stories or distractions. I'm OK with the pregnancy—really, I am."

Erin was a little frustrated that he thought her dream-traveler explanation was just a story to distract him. She said, "Dante, it wasn't a made-up story. I know it sounds crazy, but it's real. I swear it is."

Dante started to smile and shake his head and said, "So you expect me to believe that you're time traveling in your sleep?"

Erin felt like she was losing ground in the argument and just nodded.

Dante continued in a cynical tone, "Well, why don't you prove it and go and give an early version of yourself the winning lotto numbers?"

Erin quickly defended her new gift and said, "We are not allowed to do that."

Dante laughed and added sarcastically, "Of course not. Let me guess; you can time travel, but you can't do anything that will be able to prove that you were in a different time?"

Erin paused and, in a defeated voice, said, "I am only practicing dream travel, and I decided to travel to our first date to observe our first kiss..."

Dante was getting a little annoyed that Erin was still standing behind this ridiculous idea and said in a defiant voice, "Whatever."

Erin was tired of trying to defend the whole dream-travel thing. She was not sure if it was the pregnancy, but Erin felt like she had aged ten years in the past week with all the craziness in her life. She surrendered and walked back to the sink and finished washing her face and getting ready for bed.

Erin needed to think about something else, and planning her dream travel was a welcome distraction. She lifted the covers of the bed and snuggled under them. Then she started focusing on the date of their first kiss as if it were written in black print. Once she had focused on the date, she started to imagine the outfit she planned for this dream travel. Then she thought of Garden Street, the street she used to live on in Hoboken. Erin concentrated on fluctuating between the date and the outfit and slowly drifted off to sleep. She was tired, and sleep came as a welcome wave of comfort.

Erin had no idea how long she had been asleep, but she dreamed she was in the sanitation garage, walking toward the side door. She pushed opened the door and stepped into a dark space where she was immediately greeted with the smell of old dust and moisture. The room had a cement floor, red brick walls, and only one lightbulb to illuminate the whole room. As her eyes adjusted to the dim lighting, she realized she was in the basement of the building in Hoboken that she used to live in. Erin was looking at the fenced-in, cubed area that was designated as her storage area when she realized that, even in this dim lighting, her vision was too clear and the surroundings were too real to be only a dream.

Erin knew she was dream traveling. The apartment in Hoboken where she had lived was in a building that was over one hundred years old, and the wooden steps from the basement to the first floor must have been the original stairs because they creaked and groaned painfully as she stepped on each one. Erin knew the repercussions of coming across the earlier version of herself, and she cautiously opened the basement door and peeked into the front foyer of the building. The foyer was completely empty, so she quickly slipped across the foyer and out into the street where she strolled about four buildings down from her apartment and sat on a bench.

Erin did not have to wait long, because it was only a few minutes before she heard the engine of Dante's motorcycle coming down the street. She quickly pulled the brim of the baseball hat so low that she could barely see and no one would be able to get a clear image of her face. She caught a glimpse of herself walking out of her old building and walking toward Dante on the street. She saw a huge grin spread across her younger face as Dante took off his helmet and waved.

Amazingly, even years later, the DT version of Erin had to smile remembering the pleasure of seeing Dante looking so dangerous in his motorcycle gear. Erin watched and kept about five hundred feet behind the couple as they walked together to a restaurant about two blocks away. Erin knew that she would be noticed if she got too close to the couple, so she stayed outside as they had a nice dinner inside. She passed the time reading a newspaper that had been discarded on a bench.

Erin read through the old news stories and found it bittersweet to read New York City news from prior to 9/11. It was unsettling knowing that, at this point in time, terrorists were planning the horrible attacks on the United States that would take place less than a year later. Erin wondered if, as a dream traveler, she could do anything to reverse that horrible tragedy. She made a mental note to ask Sienna about it.

When it was too dark to read, Erin got up and went back to her building to find a good lookout place to wait for the return of her former self and Dante. She found a brownstone building two houses down on the opposite side of the street with thick cement pillars as a stair railing, and she sat on the steps, hiding most of her body behind one of the pillars. To anyone passing by, Erin would look like a local citizen sitting on her front steps and getting some fresh air. Erin's building was on the corner of Tenth Street and Garden Street, and from where she was sitting, she would only see the couple returning once they passed the corner of her building.

As Erin stared at her building, she saw the younger version of herself and Dante walk hand-in-hand past the corner of the building and to the front door. Erin happily realized that dream travel gave her the unique ability to watch, and almost relive, this joyful moment in her past. The recent inconvenience of becoming a dream traveler was worth the trouble just to have this opportunity to reexperience this moment. As Erin leaned forward, she stared intently and analyzed the younger version of herself and Dante.

She could barely hear them talking, but Erin remembered the words that had transpired. Just as the young couple got to the front door, Mrs. Miller, the elderly woman who lived on the first floor of

Erin's building, arrived at the door, too. Mrs. Miller was pulling her foldable metal shopping cart, filled with groceries. Without hesitation, Dante greeted Mrs. Miller and helped her lift the cart over the threshold of the doorway. Mrs. Miller was obviously impressed with Dante's courtesy and smiled and secretly nodded at Erin. Erin remembered that she too was impressed with this gentlemanly gesture.

The dream-traveler version of Erin continued to watch intensely and saw that, as soon as the door closed, Dante returned to his former spot in front of the younger version of herself. Dante looked into the younger Erin's eyes and said, "I had a wonderful time tonight. Would it be OK if we did this again?"

Erin blushed and said in a warm voice, "I would like that a lot." They paused for a second, and she made the first move to say good-bye by moving forward to embrace Dante with a good-bye hug. Dante raised his arms to return the embrace, but—in the last second, as their heads should have passed each other in a regular hug—he made the daring move of stealing a kiss.

The DT version of Erin stopped breathing as she watched the scene and relived it in her memory at the same time. She remembered how she was shocked by the surprise kiss, and then she was shocked by how amazing the kiss made her feel. She remembered that when she felt Dante's soft lips join their two bodies, she was hit with a wave of euphoria equivalent to the rush she felt when she saw fireworks up close.

Dante pulled her close, and she in turn pressed against his body and encircled her arms around his back, pulling him closer. Both Dante's and Erin's lips moved ever so slightly in the tiniest of movements, but it created the most amazing feeling. Pulses of pleasure coursed between them as if their lips had been designed for only each other. The kiss lasted less than a minute, but the memory of the sensations it generated would last a lifetime.

The dream-traveler version of Erin was hit with the need for oxygen, and she finally took a deep breath. She saw that the younger version of herself and Dante had gently pulled apart but were still holding hands. She saw that her face was flushed, and her eyes were glazed over. She also noticed that Dante was staring intently into the eyes of the younger version of Erin, and he had a huge smile on his face. The younger Erin couldn't resist smiling back at him.

Erin watched and remembered as Dante leaned in and whispered, "I better go before Mrs. Miller has a heart attack!"

The younger Erin giggled as she glanced over her shoulder and saw Mrs. Miller peeking through her blinds and watching the young couple. She regretfully let go of Dante's hands and stepped toward the front door of her building. As young Erin turned to wave good-bye one last time, Dante never took his eyes off her as he retreated toward his motorcycle. Erin had a smile on her face as she went into her building in an elated stupor.

Erin knew that she would be waking up soon, since she had spent several hours on this dream travel. She needed to retreat to an area where no one would see her disappear. Erin had forgotten to add her building keys to her planning, so there would be no way to get back through the front door of her building and into the basement. However, her building was probably not the best place to go with Mrs. Miller snooping so much. She walked down the street and found a large, dark doorway tucked under a set of entry stairs to a brown-stone building. Erin tucked herself into the dark alcove, closed her eyes, and quietly reveled in the wonderful feelings she had just re-lived. When Erin opened her eyes, she was lying in bed next to Dante. She tried to fall back to sleep, knowing that in less than an hour she would be awakened by the alarm clock.

12

E rin quickly leaned over, shut the alarm clock off, and rolled back onto her side to stare at her sleeping husband. She admired his beautiful Roman features and thought of how peaceful and relaxed he looked when he was sleeping. She said a silent prayer of thanks for such a wonderful man and wonderful life. Erin knew that her life was not always easy; however, the wonderful moments outweighed the difficult ones, and for that she was blessed.

Erin got out of bed and went into the bathroom. As she showered she noticed that her chest was extra tender this morning. She realized this must be due to her pregnancy and smiled, thinking about the life growing inside her. It felt too good to be true to be able to have a baby, and Erin was almost afraid to start dreaming about what her baby would be like. She was well aware that it was not uncommon to have a miscarriage in this early stage, and she was afraid that falling in love with her baby too early would make a possible miscarriage that much harder to deal with.

Erin continued through her normal morning routine of carrying up the coffee for Dante and herself and going through what they would be doing that day. Erin was filled with euphoric feelings from her dream-travel experience and figured she would probably have a silly grin on her face for the rest of the day. She didn't mind the distraction and was happy to have relived such a wonderful moment in her life.

Erin went downstairs and greeted Sandra with a cheery, "Good morning." Erin wondered if a good mood could be contagious because Sandra smiled and returned her good morning. They climbed into the car together and headed to school. Minutes later, Sandra really shocked Erin when she said thank you as she climbed out of the car.

Erin said, "You're welcome. Have a good day!" She wondered if Sandra had finally reached the end of her "alien" phase.

When Erin got to work, Molly commented, "Well, someone is happy this morning! What happened? Tell me why you're smiling like a clown."

Erin laughed and said, "I'm just having a good day." She changed the subject by saying, "What time is our meeting this morning?"

Molly's face changed, and she responded, "What meeting?"

"Our budget meeting."

Molly suddenly looked fearful, and she said, "Oh no, I have to present my forecast for the clinical supplies, and I totally forgot." She ran back to her desk and started plugging away at her computer.

"Let me know if you need any help," Erin said.

Molly nodded but kept her focus on her computer screen as she typed rapidly.

Erin continued walking to her desk and saw a Post-it Note stuck on her computer monitor from Sarah, the study director of her clinical trial. The note said, "Please come and see me when you can." Erin wondered what Sarah wanted as she put her bag down and headed toward Sarah's office. Sarah's door was open, and as soon as Erin stood in the doorway, Sarah greeted her energetically. "I am glad you are here!" Erin smiled and entered the office.

Sarah was in her midforties and had a robust body frame with short, thick legs and large, pudgy arms. She had short, fiery red hair that she curled away from her face and large blackish-brown eyes. Sarah did everything to the extreme—from applying too much purple eye shadow to drinking too much caffeine. It was only a quarter to eight, but Sarah had an empty large iced-coffee cup on her desk and was sipping coffee from a sixteen-ounce cup. As a result of all that caffeine, Sarah spoke at lightning speed. She quickly briefed Erin that the president of Kaso Pharmaceuticals was coming for a surprise visit to their department, and everyone was going crazy trying to put together updated project presentations. Sarah asked Erin to create a PowerPoint presentation on their study and to have it ready for her to review by the end of the day.

Erin canceled her meetings for the rest of the day and began culminating the update numbers needed for her presentation. Her good mood dissolved under the pressure, and she spent the rest of the day at her desk creating and editing her presentation.

Molly looked exhausted when she came over to Erin's desk in the afternoon. She sighed and said, "I finished the forecast. Do you need help with anything?"

Molly volunteered to proofread the presentation. Erin completed the presentation with Molly's help and e-mailed it to Sarah by a quarter to five. Erin stopped by Sarah's office to confirm that she received the e-mailed PowerPoint and couldn't help smiling when she saw Sarah still sipping coffee.

As soon as Erin stepped in the doorway, Sarah said in her typical, rapid fashion, "Thank you so much for taking care of that presentation. It looks great, and I really appreciate it."

"No problem. Do you need help with anything else?"

"No, I think we're all set. Have a good night."

Erin walked back to her desk and wondered how the megadoses of caffeine were affecting Sarah's overall health.

Erin spent a few minutes catching up on her e-mail messages. But before she had finished opening her e-mails, she received a text from Sandra asking to be picked up from school. Erin rushed to pack her bag and then hurried out of the office without saying good-bye to anyone. She knew that Molly and Debra were going to tease her for making what they had coined an "Irish exit"—leaving without saying good-bye to anyone—but she was running behind schedule. She would just have to deal with the teasing when she came back to work tomorrow.

Erin followed her typical routine of picking up Sandra from school and going to the supermarket to buy food for dinner. She was a little surprised when Sandra turned off her iPod when Erin parked at the grocery store and asked if it was OK if she went shopping with Erin. Erin quickly replied, "Yes, that would be nice."

Erin wondered what was going on with Sandra. She had been extra nice that morning, and now she wanted to spend time with Erin in the grocery store. As they wandered around the store, Erin noticed that Sandra was being extremely helpful, and although Erin loved this helpful wonderful version of Sandra, she was almost certain that something must be wrong. Erin finished shopping and decided to talk to Sandra once they got back home.

They arrived home before Dante, so they both carried bags of groceries into the kitchen. When Sandra started to put the groceries away, Erin couldn't hold back anymore. "Sandra, is everything OK?"

Sandra hesitated, and her eyes glazed over as she slowly said, "Yes, everything is fine."

Erin could tell that Sandra was not all right, and she asked in a soft whisper, "Is everything OK at school?"

Sandra looked like a dam about to burst. Her face grew very red, and her eyes welled up with tears as she cried, "I don't know anymore!"

Erin dropped the bag she was holding on the kitchen counter and quickly hugged Sandra.

Sandra started sobbing and stuttering as she tried to explain what was bothering her at school. She cried, "I don't know what wha... wha...happened...Nicole and I are friends, but Nicole is also friends with Leslie—which is fine. But Nicole and Leslie had a fight last weekend, and now Leslie isn't talking to us, and Nicole said Leslie was bossing her around and told her not to be friends with me...But I didn't do anything wrong! For some reason Leslie hates me, and now she hates that Nicole chose me over her and is really upset."

Sandra hiccupped and sobbed at the same time as she tried to catch her breath. "It isn't fair. I didn't do anything wrong, but Leslie is starting to spread rumors about me. I found out today that she told some people that I was a slut and was basically sleeping with the football team." Sandra exploded into uncontrollable sobs on Erin's shoulder.

Erin's reaction shocked her because she was instantly filled with anger and wanted to smack Leslie for hurting Sandra.

Erin reigned in her emotions and tried to soothe Sandra by saying, "Shhh…it's going to be OK. Girls can be horrible to each other sometimes for no reason. Sometimes they are jealous, and other times they have trouble at home and try to take it out on someone else. Unfortunately, dealing with situations like this is part of life, and the best thing you can do is to take the high road and do the right thing.

"Talk to Leslie alone, and let her know that you have heard that she is saying negative things about you. Let her know that it has to stop. We don't know what has happened in Leslie's life that has made her do something this horrible, but she has probably experienced something bad and is suffering. You have to remember that when you confront her.

"The next thing you have to do is to let her know that you're not her punching bag and that she can't come after you. Tell her that whatever she has said about you is done, but it's over, and she will not be saying anything negative about you again. If you can say all of that with confidence and without raising Leslie's defenses, you should be able to put a stop to it. However, at the same time, you cannot seek revenge for what was already done, or this will never end."

Erin hugged Sandra for a while and knew this was just a normal rite of passage of being a teenage girl. Until that moment she had forgotten how hard it was to be a girl in high school, and she felt a little guilty about complaining about Sandra's mood swings. Erin was also very surprised how this experience had made her maternal "claws" come out. She had felt a primal need to protect her stepdaughter.

Sandra's sobs slowed then stopped, and she and Erin slowly made dinner together. When Dante walked in from work, he was happily puzzled when he saw Erin and Sandra working so well together, but he just smiled and enjoyed their dinner together.

When they were getting ready to go to bed, Dante said to Erin, "What happened to Sandra? I am happy she was being so nice, but something is definitely different with her."

Erin explained the whole situation to Dante, and he said, "Girls are so different from boys. I might be getting old, but this would never happen with the guys I went to school with."

Erin nodded and said, "You're right. I guess being a teenage girl is very different from being a teenage boy. I just wish we could protect her from all of this nonsense, but we can't. I think all we can do is to teach her how to handle difficult situations to the best of her ability."

Dante nodded in agreement as he brushed his teeth, and they both quietly finished getting ready for bed.

As Erin crawled into bed and pulled the sheets up, she remembered that she would be summoned tonight and that she should focus on what she should wear. She closed her eyes and thought about a cute pink dress that she had seen a woman on a sitcom wearing when she had flipped through the TV channels that night. She focused on what she would look like in that outfit as she fell asleep.

13

E rin had grown used to the slipping feeling of being summoned and was not startled as she touched down in the field outside of Sienna's house. She quickly noted that she liked the pink dress and walked up Sienna's stairs. Erin again admired the beautiful setting as she climbed. She couldn't imagine a more perfect paradise to have as a home.

Erin walked over to the garden, where Sienna greeted her with a hug, and they both sat down in the cushy chairs. Erin quickly updated Sienna on the details of her dream travel. Sienna questioned her about the technical details of where she appeared, if she had interacted with anyone, and how she had returned from her dream travel. As Sienna listened to Erin, she turned on her laptop and the projector. The screen lit up, and Sienna started the evening's lesson.

"I'm glad everything went well last night, but there are a few more major things you need to learn about dream travel. I probably should have taught you this before your first dream-travel experience, but it's important that you know how to return from dream travel when you choose to instead of having to wait until you wake up for the day."

A slide titled *Terminating Dream Travel* appeared, and Sienna continued. "As you discovered when you saw your father on your first dream travel, if you get upset and cry, you will wake up. For some reason, crying wakes most people from dreaming."

Erin nodded as she remembered her first dream-travel experience and how she had cried herself awake after seeing her father and Uncle Sean together.

Sienna continued, "Unfortunately, you know how hard it is to make yourself cry on demand when you are awake, and it's even harder when you're dream traveling; however, another method is to try to yawn. In a similar way to when you're on a plane, yawning can cause your ears to pop, and that usually brings you back from dream traveling. Obviously, it's imperative that you immediately try to come back from dream traveling if you are near a Terrent."

Erin nodded thoughtfully and asked, "What does it feel like when you're hijacked by a Terrent?"

Sienna answered, "Thankfully, I have never been hijacked. But from what others have told me, they have a horrible feeling of foreboding when a Terrent is near, and once they are hijacked, they feel even worse. Some have said that they feel like all their energy is drained from their bodies, and they feel like zombies. Others have said it is like an out-of-body experience where they have no control over their dream travel, and they can only sit by and watch."

Erin shuddered with fear as she digested the information. Sienna noticed and said, "Hopefully, you'll never have to experience that. There's no need to worry. You'll be under observation for a little while until you get the hang of how to dream travel. I knew your dream travel last night was personal, so I didn't directly observe you. However, I was about a block away from you at all times to make sure no Terrents were in the area. I will continue to stay in the periphery of your dream-travel experiences until you feel comfortable on your own."

Erin felt a wave of relief and smiled. She hadn't realized how tense the conversation had made her until she felt the muscles in her neck and shoulders relax. She was grateful that Sienna would be there as her backup until she was ready to go solo.

Sienna moved to the next slide, *Garan Safety*. "As we've said before, there are currently six known Garans in the world. All Garans have to maintain extreme security measures at all times. Some of these measures include that we all live in secluded areas, typically on islands. Islands offer the ability to control the influx of visitors, since people have to arrive by boat or plane. In addition, we're able to manipulate some of the resources on the islands, such as fluoridating the water and sometimes the local food supply.

"Here on Dominica, the local water is fluoridated, and most of the local produce has been genetically designed to include fluoride. My home is elevated, and visitors have to walk through the mist as they come up the stairs. That water has a high concentration of fluoride that would inhibit any Terrent's ability to hijack a dream traveler or a Garan. In addition, I have a state-of-the-art security system with twenty-four-hour-a-day security guard coverage."

Erin relived her approach to Sienna's home and marveled at how well thought-out these security measures were. Things like the water misters, that Erin had assumed were luxurious amenities in a tropical climate, actually served an important security purpose. Erin wondered if she would ever stop being amazed at the intricacies of the dream-traveler world.

Sienna continued her lesson and said, "You know that dream travelers and Garans can only dream travel while they are sleeping. As you're learning, dream travelers can only dream travel back in time. Garans can dream travel back and forward in time. Terrents can only hijack a dream traveler or Garan when he or she is in the dream-traveler state. Although the awake Garans and awake dream travelers cannot be hijacked by Terrents, our security is very important."

Sienna raised her eyebrows and hypothesized, "A Terrent could potentially physically kidnap a dream traveler and somehow force him or her to fall asleep and dream travel to a previous day at a location that the Terrent was at the time. Once the Terrent hijacked the dream traveler in the dream-travel state, they would be able to go back in time."

Sienna paused and said, "Similarly, a Terrent could potentially physically kidnap a Garan and somehow force him or her to fall asleep and dream travel to a previous day at a location that the Terrent was at the time. Once the Terrent hijacked the Garan in the dream-travel state, they'd be able to go back and forward in time. Dream-traveler safety is important, and the Garan's ability to travel backward and forward in time makes us extremely valuable to Terrents; thus, Garan safety is paramount. That's why Garans have such intracate security measures in place, and we ask that all our dream travelers maintain their security at all times.

"I doubt you have heard the story yet, but my birth was one of the turning points in history for all Terrents. My mother is a Terrent, and my birth was the first recorded case of a Terrent not only giving birth to a dream traveler but also giving birth to a Garan. It could have been an unimaginable boon for all Terrents, and obviously, it was a landmark in history for both dream travelers and Terrents."

Erin was shocked by this revelation, which must have been obvious from the look on her face. Sienna smiled calmly and nodded slightly.

"My mother came from a family of Terrents, and she chose to leave that life at the age of fifteen when she struck out on her own. My mother had been working as a waitress in New York City when my father seduced her. My father was a rogue dream traveler and a successful investment banker. My mother was young, and she stupidly fell in love with my father—not knowing that he was a dream traveler or that he was engaged. My father decided to let her know that their 'fling' was over when he was getting married the next day. Obviously, my mother was heartbroken. My father never found out that my mother was a Terrent or that she had his child."

Sienna paused before she continued. "She kept working as a waitress up until the day she gave birth to me. When I was born with my Garan birthmark, my mother was terrified that one of her fellow Terrent family members would discover that she had given birth to a Garan. She couldn't imagine the torment that I would endure in the Terrent world as their personal Garan transporter, and she decided to seek out the DTC. She waited until she heard the familiar ringing of a dream traveler, and instead of hijacking her, she pleaded with the dream traveler to speak to the DTC. The DTC quickly followed the normal steps of a new Garan birth and placed me in a secure Garan setting. I was sent to live with the Garan, Rayna, and she raised me as her own."

Erin gasped and said, "The DTC took you from your birth mother just because she was a Terrent?"

Sienna looked tired and calmly responded, "The DTC didn't take me from my mother because she was a Terrent; they took me away because all Garan babies are placed with other Garans. That is the only place they are safe. Even if my mother had been a dream traveler, I still would have been placed with Rayna until I reached adulthood."

Erin was shocked by this fact and felt sorry for all the mothers who didn't get to raise their own children. Sienna paused and then said, "My mother understood it was for my own safety, and I still see her from time to time. In fact, lately we have been talking almost daily because of you. My birth mother is Anna."

Erin was speechless. She had always had a nagging feeling of familiarity when she was with Sienna, and now it all made sense. How could she have missed the similar almond-shaped brown eyes and the identical mannerisms shared by Anna and Sienna? They both had curvy figures, and although Anna's figure had softened around the middle with time, it was easy to imagine that she must have looked like Sienna twenty years ago. It seemed so obvious now that Erin knew the truth. She felt like an idiot for not realizing it before. She covered her confusion and said, "That must have been hard for Anna to give up her child."

Sienna nodded in agreement and said, "I am sure it was, but she had grown up hearing her own Terrent family members talk about how they would use a Garan if they were ever able to capture one. She made the right choice to give me to Rayna to be raised under full Garan protection. She did stay with me at Rayna's home in the Philippians for several years, but after a while she felt she couldn't go on living off Rayna's generosity. My mother went back to school and became a schoolteacher. She got a job in the United States and left Rayna's home when I turned thirteen. From that point forward, she would fly back to the Philippians and visit me once a year over the Christmas holidays."

Sienna repositioned herself in the chair and reached over and shut the projector off. She turned back to Erin and said, "I think we have covered a lot tonight. In fact, I think we have finished most of the classroom lessons at this point. I am going to let the DTC know that you're ready to start receiving assignments."

Erin's eyes widened as she nodded, trying to get used to the fact that she was ready to start working on DTC assignments.

Sienna quickly added, "Remember, I will be with you on your first assignments until you feel comfortable on your own. Catch up on your rest this weekend, and by five o'clock on Sunday evening, you will receive an e-mail message with the date, time, and place where you're supposed to dream travel. The message will have pictures of the outfit you should wear, the exact location you should appear, the person or people you should observe, and what information the DTC is specifically looking for. Try to fall asleep by ten o'clock, if possible, to ensure you have plenty of time to complete your assignment. Also, I will summon you again on Monday night to discuss how your first assignment went."

Erin nodded and said, "OK. I'm a little nervous, but I feel better knowing that you will be there also."

Sienna smiled and said, "You're going to do great."

Erin couldn't help feeling a little excited with this new role. It was as if she were getting to live the life of a secret spy at night.

Sienna stood up and said, "Well, I'd better let you get some sleep."

Erin stood up too and hugged Sienna good-bye. She moved to the lounge chair, closed her eyes, and allowed Sienna to send her back to her bed. Erin opened her eyes a fraction and saw that it was still dark outside her bedroom window. She cuddled closer to Dante and fell back asleep.

14

E rin heard the alarm clock and started rubbing her eyes. As she climbed out of bed, she was thinking about what her day at work was going to be like. Then she remembered that the president of Kaso Pharmaceuticals was coming to the office today, and she felt a wave of dread at the thought of what she knew would be a hectic day at work. She went through her normal morning-coffee ritual a little faster than usual and rushed to get to work early to make sure she was ready for anything that might come up.

As Erin walked into the office, she saw Debra hurrying toward Sarah's office with a large cup of coffee from the cafeteria, and Erin wondered how many cups of coffee Sarah had already drunk. Erin quickly walked over to her desk and scanned her e-mails. She found numerous e-mail meeting invitations for that morning and afternoon. It appeared that the morning would be filled with meetings to rehearse the presentations, and this afternoon there would be a mandatory three-hour company meeting, where the study teams would present their study progress updates to the president.

Erin made it through her morning meetings, providing study details that were not included in the presentation and watching Sarah rehearse. Sarah's one flaw during the rehearsal was that she was speaking too fast, and after some persuasion Sarah agreed to avoid coffee for the next few hours before she had to give the study presentation. Molly, Erin, and Sarah had a working lunch of sandwiches in a conference room while they put the final touches on the presentation.

It was a lot of hard work, but Erin really enjoyed working on Sarah's study team. Sarah had the same old-fashioned work ethic Erin had, so she never backed away from a challenge and was well respected as a good team leader. Erin felt that she was lucky to be part of such a close-knit team where everyone pitched in, worked hard, and enjoyed what they accomplished.

Their presentation at the afternoon meeting went flawlessly. Sarah did a superb job and clearly impressed the president with the study's progress and the speed at which the study was enrolling participants. Mark Williams, the president of Kaso Pharmaceuticals, was a balding, obese, middle-aged man with a type A personality. He was constantly driving to improve processes and to produce new products for the company. He studied Sarah with his intense brown eyes and nodded in agreement as she provided the update and explained the next steps that she had planned for the study.

Most Kaso employees acted similarly to Erin during the three-hour meeting: they sat politely and quietly and never ventured to ask a question or make a comment. The one exception was Ronan McKenna, who, in an effort to look intelligent, would ask questions and proceed to answer his own questions. He was obviously trying to impress the president, but Erin noticed many people in the room were rolling their eyes when they did not think anyone was looking.

At the conclusion of Sarah's presentation, Ronan somehow managed to redirect the conversation back to his male-pattern baldness study, and he took the opportunity to speak of his many successful interventions and accomplishments. Unfortunately, Mark Williams fell for Ronan's polished charm and was nodding happily as he listened to Ronan sing his own praise. The meeting ended with Mark congratulating Ronan for a great job, and everyone filed out of the conference room in awed and a little disgusted that Ronan had managed to steal Sarah's limelight for himself.

Erin saw Sarah file back to her office with her head down in defeat. The meeting had gone longer than expected, and when Erin returned to her desk, she realized that Sandra had texted more than ten minutes ago asking for a ride home. Erin hesitated, and then she walked over to Sarah's office to check on her. Sarah had her back to Erin and was sniffling as she reached toward the tissue box on the shelf situated on the back wall of her office. Erin knew that Sarah would be very embarrassed if anyone witnessed this crying episode, so she quietly stepped backward and walked back to her desk. As Erin packed up her briefcase to go home, anger toward Ronan McKenna boiled up inside her. Sarah was part of Erin's work family, and she couldn't help feeling protective of her.

Erin pushed through the rest of her evening routine of picking up Sandra, stopping at the grocery store, and making dinner. When they had finished eating Erin told Dante what had happened that day. As they cleaned up and loaded the dishes into the dishwasher, she explained how well Sarah did at the meeting and how Ronan had upstaged her.

Dante just shook his head and said, "Try to stay away from Ronan if you can; he sounds like a real snake."

Erin nodded in agreement and said, "I will. Luckily he works on another study, and I don't have to interact with him that often."

Sandra walked into the kitchen and said, "Nicole's mom is outside. She said that she would drive Nicole and me to the mall and pick us up around ten." Dante and Erin both nodded in response as they followed Sandra to the front door and waved to Nicole's mom.

"Please, be careful," said Erin.

"I will," answered Sandra, and she climbed into the back seat of her friend's SUV.

Dante closed the front door and started walking back to the kitchen. "Has anything happened with that girl Sandra was upset about?" he asked.

"Sandra said that she confronted Leslie and that she thinks she surprised her and caught her off guard. She said that it was hard, but she thinks that Leslie will leave her alone now—or at least she hopes so."

Dante shook his head in confusion and asked, "Are you ready to do this all over again?"

Erin knew he was referring to the pregnancy and said, "Of course. It will be different. I think it can only be easier than being a step-mom. As a natural mother, I won't have to work around the balancing act of trying to discipline and yet not be seen as the evil stepmother."

Dante walked over and put his arms around Erin and said, "I guess you're right. You know I really do appreciate everything you do for Sandra. You sacrifice more than her biological mother does, and I just hope that someday Sandra realizes how lucky she is to have you in her life."

Erin choked back a tear and kissed Dante softly. She felt so lucky to have found her true love. They might disagree from time to time, but Erin couldn't imagine her life without Dante and never wanted to be without him.

They enjoyed their typical Friday night activity of making pop-corn and watching a movie together. Erin cuddled up next to Dante on the couch and sat back to watch a DVD that they hadn't really heard any reviews about. Erin was happily surprised that it turned out to be a hysterical comedy with a lot of extremely dry humor. They laughed so hard that they both teared up at some parts, and by the end of the movie, Erin's stomach actually hurt from laughing so hard. It was exactly what Erin needed after a long week.

Sandra came home on time, smiled at Erin and Dante's state of giggles, said good night, and went to bed. Dante and Erin continued to giggle as they got ready for bed and quoted their favorite lines from the movie. They cuddled up in bed and relaxed into a state of content-ment. Erin snuggled her head into the curve of Dante's neck and took a deep breath. She loved how Dante smelled. There was something about his natural scent that enticed her to him and made her feel com-plete a the same time. She fell asleep with a smile on her face.

Erin woke up after a night of good, old-fashioned sleep to the sun streaming in through the sides of the shades and felt wonderfully rested. Dante was already out of bed, and she smelled the scent of pancakes cooking downstairs. Dante spent so much time working long hours during the week that he usually tried to make everyone breakfast on the weekends. Erin smiled as she walked into the kitchen and found pancakes on the table and a cup of coffee waiting for her.

The morning was going well until the mail came at noon, and Dante opened the envelope with Sandra's report card. Sandra had sworn for weeks that she was doing well in school, but her report card told a different story. She had received a D in biology. Dante was irate. Sandra was in the kitchen trying to explain that it was because the teacher hated her, but Dante said, "I just don't understand. I'm a doctor, and of all subjects, I could have easily tutored you in biology. Why did you lie and say you were doing well in all your classes?"

Sandra was crying and said, "I failed an exam, and I thought that I could get my biology grade back up on my own."

"No one is perfect, and I'm not upset that you were having trouble in biology and failed a test," Dante said. "But I am extremely upset that you didn't ask for help. I've told you a million times that lying only leads to more problems. This is unacceptable and has to stop. You know our rule; no more texting until you have at least Cs and better on your report card. Can I trust you not to text?"

Sandra quickly nodded in agreement. She looked solemnly at her father and said, "I am going to go upstairs and study right now." Then she gathered her backpack from the front foyer and went upstairs to her bedroom.

Dante was in a grim mood for the rest of the day, and Erin resigned herself to the fact that the rest of the weekend was going to be bad with Dante this upset. She decided to catch up on errands and went shopping for holiday gifts. She came home around five o'clock and saw Dante sitting in the office on the first floor in front of the computer, looking even more upset than when she had left.

As soon as she walked in the front door, Dante called to Erin to come over. He pointed at the computer screen and said, "Look at this! I just accessed our cell phone account and saw this activity on Sandra's cell phone!" Erin looked at the display and saw that Sandra had managed to send over one hundred text messages in the four hours since she had agreed not to text. Erin swallowed hard and knew their weekend was going to get worse. Dante said, "Don't say anything. I'm waiting for dinner, and I'm going to see if Sandra has learned anything that you have tried to teach her about why it is always better to be honest."

Erin made dinner with a heavy heart. She was not looking forward to the conflict that might take place between Dante and Sandra. Erin lived an honest life and worked hard to avoid lying at all cost. She had learned early on that if she chose to be honest, she usually made the right decision because she would hold herself accountable for explaining her actions honestly.

They sat down for dinner together, and she immediately felt the tension in the air as the meal began. No one said a word until Erin tried to lighten the conversation by talking about the funny movie they had watched the prior evening.

Dante was not in the mood for light conversation, and he changed the topic to what was on his mind. "Sandra, have you texted on your phone this afternoon?"

The empty look in Sandra's eyes scared Erin a little. "No, not since you told me I couldn't text anymore," Sandra replied.

Dante quickly said, "So you are saying that you have not texted since you promised not to this afternoon, right?"

Sandra gave him a hollow look, swallowed, and said, "No, not since you told me not to." She then got teary-eyed and yelled, "This is so unfair! You *never* believe me!"

Dante was boiling with anger and responded, "Really? Why do you think I don't believe you?"

Sandra was sobbing by now and said, "You just never trust me! You think you are so much better than everyone else! You are so *mean* to me!"

Erin cringed and wished that she could be anywhere else besides where she was. She also felt sorry that Dante was in the middle of this situation.

Dante slowly stood up and walked over to the office on the first floor where the computer was. He calmly said, "Sandra, come over here." When Sandra joined him, Dante pointed at the computer screen and said, "How many messages have you sent in that time you just said that you *did not* text?"

Sandra was shocked that Dante had accessed the wireless account and checked on her. She continued to sob out the same phrases: "This is so unfair! You are so mean!" Erin was floored that even in this type of situation, where Sandra clearly did something wrong, lied about it, and was caught in a lie, she still had the audacity to blame it on her father.

Erin admired Dante's self-control as he said in a calm voice, "I will now cancel your text messaging with the phone company, and in addition to that, you lose all instant messaging and chat capabilities on your laptop computer as well."

Sandra ran out of the room and upstairs to her bedroom, screaming insults and crying.

Erin was stunned by the whole situation. She was shocked that Sandra had lied so freely even after all the reasons and lectures she had given her about the pitfalls of lying. Erin's parents used to have a theory about raising children. They said that, after a certain age, it was too late to change a child's behavior. Erin hoped that it wasn't too late for Sandra.

The whole weekend was ruined for everyone. Dante was upset for the rest of the evening and tossed and turned in bed all night. Erin woke up Sunday morning exhausted from Dante waking her up with his restlessness. As soon as she opened her eyes, she remembered the emotional situation they were in the midst of and decided that, since the day was going to be depressing anyway, she would clean the whole house.

Dante moped around the house, and Sandra stayed in her room except for the few brief times she ventured out for food. By the afternoon Erin was actually looking forward to her first dream-travel experience as an escape from her current situation. She wondered what type of assignment she would receive and if she would be able to dream travel and carry out her assignment properly.

Erin started checking her e-mail at four o'clock, and at exactly 4:55 p.m., she received an e-mail from S.Goodman@dmail.com with "No Subject" written in the subject line. Erin quickly opened the e-mail and saw what looked like an excerpt from a website listing information about a day care center in Little Falls, New Jersey:

Business: Little Hands Day Care
Date: February 24, 1991, 10:20 a.m.
Address: 334 Main Street, Little Falls, NJ
Weather: Sunny and 42 degrees Fahrenheit

The second part of the excerpt said…

Sit on the bench at the bus stop across the street from the day care center playground. Look at Jerry Lamar at 10:20 a.m. on February 24, 1991.

Three photos were attached to the e-mail, and Erin opened and studied each one. The first was a picture of a mannequin wearing a knit cap, black sunglasses, and an outfit of jeans, a red turtleneck sweater, and a black leather, waist-length jacket. The second photo was a picture of a young boy who was probably around two years old. He had a round face, adorable rosy cheeks, blond hair, and blue eyes. The name listed under the picture was Jerry Lamar. The third photo was of a garbage Dumpster next to the day care center, and the caption under the picture said, "Appear and return from outside the rear section of this Dumpster, on the side that faces the back fence."

Erin was a little apprehensive about the whole assignment. She tried to be optimistic by thinking of the bright side; at least she didn't have to appear and disappear from inside the Dumpster. Then a flood of questions went through her mind. Why did the message say that she should look at little Jerry Lamar? Why didn't the message tell her what to look for?

However, Erin gradually became a little excited about her first real dream-traveler assignment. She was nervous that she would make a mistake and somehow mess it up, but she was also looking forward to being able to accomplish a dream-travel assignment for the DTC. She had a sense of achievement and purpose that came from completing her training and being able to do an actual job for the DTC. Now she was receiving work, she felt like she was really part of the dream-traveler society.

Erin was so distracted by thinking about her new assignment and wondering how it would turn out that the rest of her Sunday evening flew by. Before she knew it, she was lying in bed, preparing her mind for dream travel. As Erin closed her eyes and fell asleep, she alternated her concentration from the image of 10:20 a.m. on February 24, 1991, the image of where she should appear, and the image of the outfit she was supposed to wear. Then she fell into a deep sleep.

15

Erin recognized the smell of the New York City sanitation garage before she opened her eyes and saw the dark, sunless room. She was standing in front of the side door, and she immediatley reached forward and opened it. As Erin stepped through the doorway, her first thought was that it was cold. She found herself standing next to a Dumpster, looking out at a chain-link fence on a bright, crisp, sunny day. She looked around and confirmed that no one had seen her appear. Erin saw the side of the red brick building on her left and a chain-link fence on her right as she faced the parking lot in front of the building.

Erin slowly moved along the side of the building until she reached the front corner and glanced at the parking lot. There was a black Honda Accord and a blue Ford Taurus parked in the lot, but no one was outside. Erin quickly ran diagonally across the parking lot and stopped at the street. She waited for a couple cars to pass before crossing the street and walking toward the bus stop. Erin was relieved that the bus stop was empty, and she sat down on the bench. She was just in time to see two teachers with a group of at least ten toddlers pour out the side door of the building into the fenced-off playground directly across from the bus stop. Erin felt the coldness of the metal bench penetrate through her jeans to the back of her legs and shivered as the chill went through her.

Within seconds of the children appearing, Erin identified Jerry Lamar in the group. She watched him pull away from the other children that were playing on the bouncy horses and turn and stare directly at her. His expression was serious, and he did not take his eyes off Erin for a second. The teachers were busy talking to each other and did not notice Jerry start to walk away from the other children and toward the chain-link fence of the playground.

Erin began to fear for his safety as he clung to the fence and then started to slowly climb the four-foot-high chain-link fence. Since the fence was twice his height, the process was slow, and he had only one arm over the top of the fence before the young blond teacher yelped, *"Jerry, no!"* She ran to him and pulled him from the fence. The teacher was obviously surprised and was saying something about a "time-out" as she held his hand and walked him inside. The whole time she was marching him inside, Jerry was staring back at Erin and pulling with all his strength against the teacher, still trying to walk toward the fence. Within seconds he was back inside the building, and the other teacher was busy watching the remaining toddlers play.

Erin was thinking about what she had just witnessed when she felt a second, stronger wave of chills run though her. At the same time, a black BMW 740 pulled into the day care center parking lot, and a short, stocky woman in her late thirties, with a bob of short, bleach-blond hair stepped out of the car, closed the car door, and started toward the day care center. Suddenly, she paused, turned on her heel, and started walking directly toward Erin.

The chills Erin felt intensified drastically, and a wave of foreboding crashed into her as she sat on the bench, frozen in shock. This was a Terrent approaching her. Finally, Erin's adrenaline kicked in. The woman was about twenty feet away when Erin stood up and sprinted down the street, away from the day care center.

Erin didn't know where she was going, but she knew she had to get away from this Terrent. She ran at full speed, but she was less than two hundred feet down the road when she tripped over a raised section of the sidewalk, causing her to hurtle forward. She was able to brace her hands in front of her to break her fall, but she bumped her head on the ground and immediately felt the burn of her scratched palms, along with a throbbing sensation on her forehead where it had hit the sidewalk. Erin quickly pushed herself onto her knees and then onto her feet. She looked back and saw that the Terrent woman was running after her and was only about fifty feet behind her. Erin heard the roar of an engine before she saw the gray van coming down the road. The van came to a halt right next to Erin a second later, with the side door wide open.

To Erin's surprise Sienna was in the driver's seat and yelled, "Get in!"

Erin jumped into the back as Sienna slammed the gas pedal. At the end of the block, Erin looked back through the rear window and saw the Terrent woman running back toward her car. Erin reached over and closed the van door as Sienna quickly turned onto a busy four-lane street. Sienna was driving at the forty-five-miles-an-hour speed limit, and they had blended in with the other traffic before Erin finally started to calm down from her adrenaline rush.

Sienna glanced back at Erin and said, "Sit up here in the passenger's seat. She's not going to be able to find us now." Erin obediently climbed into the passenger's seat and locked her seat belt. Sienna looked over at Erin and said, "Are you OK?"

Erin nodded, looked down at the scratches on the palms of her hands, and said, "Yes, just a few scratches."

"Don't worry. The bruise starting on your forehead will not be there when you wake up."

Erin reached up and rubbed the bump that was growing on her forehead. Sienna drove silently for another minute and studied the street signs. She made a right-hand turn down a quieter street and then a quick left into the driveway of a small red Cape Cod cottage. She pushed the button of a garage door remote that was clipped to the visor above her head, and the garage door opened. Sienna pulled into the garage, turned off the van, and pushed the button of the garage door remote again. When the garage door closed, Sienna clicked open her seat belt and turned to face Erin.

"We will review everything that you just experienced tomorrow night when I summon you to my place," Sienna said. "Since you dream traveled yourself to this time and I didn't summon you here, you have to be able to wake yourself up. I need you to start yawning and trying to pop your ears as if you're on a plane."

At that moment Erin realized the mistake she had made earlier when she ran instead of trying to wake up when the Terrent was pursuing her. She raised her eyebrows apologetically and said, "I'm sorry! I should have done that before. I was so nervous that I just starting running instead of doing what you taught me."

Sienna smiled and said in a motherly voice, "It's OK, Erin. Everyone does that the first time they experience the shock of being pursued by a Terrent. Go ahead and try to pop your ears now."

Erin sat back and purposefully yawned. Nothing happened, and she tried again. She opened her mouth wide with a dramatic yawn and felt a click in her jaw followed by a popping sensation in her ears. As she blinked her eyes, she was surrounded in sudden darkness, and she realized that she was lying on her back in her own bed. Erin was exhausted and quickly fell into a deep sleep.

16

Erin heard the alarm go off, and Dante hit the snooze button. She felt him lie back in bed and heard his breathing pattern change as he quickly fell back asleep. Erin tried to fall back asleep, but her mind began to process everything that had happened during her dream travel. She reflected on how her assignment had started out and how quickly things had changed when the Terrent arrived. Erin was upset with herself for not remembering that she should have tried to wake up by popping her ears when the Terrent appeared. For the first time, Erin was jealous of other dream travelers who had started dream traveling in their teens. She felt clumsy, slow, and old in her learning process. Erin wondered if dream traveling was something like riding a bicycle or doing a cartwheel—better learned when one is young and reckless.

Erin pulled herself out of bed and walked into the bathroom. When she looked in the mirror, she saw the bruise was gone from her forehead. She looked down at her hands and saw that the scratches on her palms were also gone. Erin was relieved the injuries were gone, but she was feeling sorry for herself as she took a shower. She tried to refocus on what her day was going to be like at work and remembered that she had her first ultrasound scheduled for noon today. Her whole mood changed, and she smiled at the thought of seeing an image of the baby.

As Dante walked sleepily into the bathroom, Erin asked, "Can you come to Dr. Ruben's office today for the ultrasound?"

Dante rubbed the sleep out of his eyes, yawned, and said, "I think so. I have a patient coming to the hospital for a procedure at eleven o'clock, but I should be able to get there."

"Good. I'll meet you in the waiting room."

Erin happily went through the rest of her morning routine and gave Dante a kiss and hug before she went downstairs. Sandra was waiting in the kitchen and had an annoyed expression on her face. Erin stayed positive and said, "Good morning."

Sandra replied quietly, "Good morning" and followed Erin to the car.

Erin had a feeling that Sandra was feeling remorseful about her outburst and decided to stay quiet on the drive. But as they pulled out of the driveway, Sandra couldn't hold in her feelings anymore. "You know it's Dad's fault, right?"

Erin felt like rolling her eyes, but she controlled herself. She calmly asked, "What do you mean?"

Sandra answered, "If Dad hadn't said I wasn't allowed to text, I wouldn't have had to lie about it."

Erin summoned all her patience and understanding and softly said, "Sandra, do you know why your dad wants you to get good grades?"

Sandra quickly answered, "Yes, so he doesn't have to be embarrassed of me in front of his friends."

Erin paused and said, "No, it's because he loves you with his whole heart and wants you to be able to go to any college you want to go to. He has been saving for your college fund since the day you were born, and he wants you to have what he didn't have when he was growing up, the chance to attend the college you choose."

Sandra sighed and said, "You don't know what it's like to be me. I have to be able to text my friends! Things have changed since you and Dad grew up. No one talks on the phone anymore. Everyone uses text messages or instant messaging to communicate. It's almost like you don't exist without those. It was hard enough being a teenager before. Now, without texting, I am going to lose my friends!"

Erin was trying to be understanding, but she couldn't quite get her mind around this younger generation. Why was it so impossible to call a friend on the phone? Erin wondered if the more material items you had in life, the more miserable you became. Erin had so little growing up. Money was always tight, and from the time she was a little girl, her father had warned her that he couldn't afford to pay for her college. In Erin's mind Sandra had won the lottery by having the ability to choose any college she wanted.

When Erin was in high school, she had loved science and animals and desperately wanted to study to be a veterinarian, but she knew that her parents couldn't afford the education. When she was seventeen, Erin surrendered her dream to be a veterinarian and chose to be a nurse. Owen McGowan wished he could have sent his children to any college, but he had been so proud when he was able to pay for Erin's much more affordable nursing school. Erin had thrown all her energy into being an exemplary nursing student and had worked hard to eventually become president of her nursing class.

Because her experience was so different than Sandra's, it was hard for Erin to understand Sandra's dilemma. She would have done anything to have the opportunities that Sandra had. Erin pushed aside these thoughts and realized that she was probably feeling what every parent feels when a child complains. Erin finally understood why parents told their children about their seemingly exaggerated hardships, such as walking barefoot in the snow, uphill both ways, to school. It was a shock to realize she had become a fully invested stepparent because she was thinking like a full-fledged parent.

Erin took a deep breath and said, "Remember how I say that lying catches up to you and gets you into more trouble than telling the truth?"

Sandra nodded and said, "I know."

"You father is really upset and rightly so. When someone lies to your face, it feels like saying that you're too dumb to know the truth.

So lying is sort of insulting someone's intelligence." Erin paused and softly added, "I know things are confusing for you right now, but you really need to start thinking about the people who love you and how they should be treated."

Sandra did not say anything, but she appeared to be taking everything in. She looked like she had surrendered her mission of justifying herself...at least for a while. Erin slowly pulled in front of Sandra's school and quietly said, "Try to have a good day."

Sandra nodded, said thanks, and got out of the car.

Erin gave up on trying to figure out a solution for the situation with Sandra and focused on everything that she needed to complete at work before she could leave to go to Dr. Ruben's office. Thankfully, traffic was light, and Erin made it to work early. She stopped at the restroom on her way in and gasped when she noticed that she had spotted blood. Erin called Dr. Ruben's office as soon as she was at her desk and was comforted a little when the nurse said that the amount of spotting she had was nothing to be worried about and that Dr. Ruben would examine her when she came in at noon for the ultrasound. The receptionist warned Erin to call back if the spotting continued.

Erin booted up her computer. She expected the day to go slowly because she already felt exhausted, physically and emotionally. She opened her e-mail and had begun to go through the thirty new messages when she saw an e-mail from the president's secretary. The message had been sent to the entire company, and the subject was "New Promotions." Erin clicked on the e-mail and saw that some changes on study teams were being announced. Then she gasped.

Ronan McKenna would be taking over as study director for her study, and Sarah had been reassigned to the regulatory submission aspect of the study! Erin could not believe this was happening. Although Ronan McKenna had no experience in oncology clinical research, somehow he must have convinced President Williams that he was the better study-director candidate.

Erin jumped up to find Sarah and bumped into Molly, who was just coming into the office for the day. Erin brought Molly up to speed on Sarah's demotion and Ronan's promotion, and they walked over to Sarah's office together. Sarah was sitting at her desk, and Erin quickly noticed that she looked awful. Her eyes were puffy, she was not wearing any makeup, and she looked like she had not gotten any sleep in days.

"Are you OK?" asked Erin.

Sarah replied, "Yes, I'm all right. I found out before I left on Friday, and I've been thinking about it all weekend. Maybe it's for the best. I mean, I would like to learn more about the regulatory submission process...and Ronan did just about perform miracles in getting his study completed..."

Erin's face reddened, and she said, "No offense, Molly, but—"

Molly quickly broke in. "Please, don't hold back because of me. I have no idea what my sister sees in Ronan, but I try to avoid talking to him at all costs."

Erin continued. "He has no oncology experience! He directed a male-pattern baldness study! This is ridiculous that at such a critical point in the study they would start a new, inexperienced study director when you're doing such a good job!"

Sarah looked drained of fight and only nodded her head in agreement.

Molly gently added, "I am so sorry, Sarah. I would much rather work for you."

Sarah looked exhausted, and Erin didn't want to bother her anymore. Erin and Molly quietly excused themselves and returned to their desks.

Erin finished going through her e-mail and was getting ready to start reviewing study data when she noticed an e-mail from Debra pop up. The department's administrative assistant had flagged it as urgent. The subject line read "Urgent Study Team Meeting." Erin saw that Ronan was holding an impromptu study-team meeting in five minutes to discuss his new role, and Sarah wasn't invited. Erin grudgingly grabbed a pen, her notebook, and her BlackBerry and walked to the conference room where the meeting was being held.

As Erin opened the door, people stopped whispering, but once they saw that she wasn't Ronan, the whispers immediately started again. She noticed about ten other people from the study team, including Molly, already waiting in the room.

"I can't believe senior management would do this to us," said the study's project planner in a hushed whisper. As Erin sat down, the whispers hushed again, and this time Ronan entered the room.

Ronan was wearing an expensive-looking black suit, a white shirt, and a blue tie. He looked perfectly groomed with his artificial tan, slicked-back hair, and exceptionally white teeth that he displayed in a fake smile. He pretended not to hear the whispers as he sat down at the head of the table and said, "Thank you all for joining me here on such short notice. As you already know, senior management has decided that I should take over the study from this point forward."

Ronan looked so satisfied and delighted with this fact that it made Erin nauseous. Ronan's cool reception was obvious, and Ronan continued, "I know that this may be upsetting to some of you because you're accustomed to Sarah directing this team, but rest assured that I plan to run this team more efficiently."

Anger boiled up inside Erin, and she heard an audible sigh from several team members. Sarah was an amazing study director! How dare Ronan try to imply that she was running things inefficiently!

Ronan adjusted his tie and said, "I have decided that we will be changing the format used to collect the study data. We will be implementing an electronic data capture instead of using paper."

Erin said in a diplomatic voice, trying to be as polite as possible, "Ronan, we actually considered using an electronic data capture system when we set up this study, but our scientific advisors warned us not to because our study sites were not ready for the technology yet, and the technology issues could delay the data collection. Therefore, the team decided to utilize paper instead of an electronic data capture."

Ronan was prepared for this objection and said, "My job is to get the study completed and data collected as soon as possible for senior management, and I think electronic data capture is the best way to proceed."

The realization that Ronan was prepared to disregard all the research and experience that had gone into the existing data-collection structure silenced Erin.She did not raise any other objections during the meeting, but several other team members brought up the negative implications that Ronan's changes would have on the study time lines and budget.

When Ronan was challenged, he answered, "Your opinions are irrelevant. I already spoke to senior management regarding all of these changes, and they agree with my plans and said we should proceed with these changes."

Erin's study team was constructed of people who brought together all their collective years of experience and knowledge of clinical operations, data management, biostatistics, and project planning. She was appalled that Ronan was disregarding all their input and suggestions and was proceeding with his own inferior ideas, which he had cunningly had approved by senior management before the meeting. Erin was also stunned that senior management was inappropriately making study-team decisions without being presented with all the information.

By the end of the meeting, Erin felt betrayed by the senior management of Kaso Pharmaceuticals and the unjust decisions they had made. First they had replaced Sarah with this inexperienced phony, Ronan McKenna, and then they fell for his scheme of disempowering the study team. Senior management was pushing the team to finish the study successfully, but they were making it more difficult to complete and creating unnecessary risk at a critical point in the study.

Erin tried to push everything from her mind and remember that it was just a job. It was hard to do that, though, because she believed the drug they were studying was going to save lives, and she knew that the clinical trial had to be done perfectly for the FDA to approve the study drug. Erin was still trying to achieve a healthy perspective when she looked down at the time and saw that the study-team meeting had taken up her entire morning. She was already supposed to be driving to Dr. Ruben's office. She grabbed her purse and let Molly know that she had to run out to a doctor's appointment and would be back in about two hours.

Erin walked into Dr. Ruben's office without a minute to spare. Dante had made time for the appointment and was already there when she arrived. Dante was sitting awkwardly in a corner chair in the waiting room. He was the only man in the room and was surrounded by several female patients of various ages and a few small children playing with coloring books in the corner. Erin felt a wave of love for Dante, knowing he had probably sped through his work at lightning speed to be able to make it here for her. She quickly walked over to him and gave him a kiss.

They walked up to the counter to tell the receptionist they had arrived. Theresa, Dr. Ruben's nurse, popped up behind the receptionist and said, "Erin, we are all set for you. Please follow me."

Erin and Dante followed Theresa down the hall. As they walked down the hallway, they passed several examination rooms, and Erin realized that she had a ringing in her ears.

"Do you hear that?" Erin whispered to Dante as they walked.

"You mean that ringing sound? Maybe it has something to do with the equipment."

The room had several metal cabinets, a door on one of the walls with a Supply Closet sign, and several machines—including one with a computer monitor-type screen attached to it. Erin knew the real reason for the ringing sounds now, and she wondered who in the building was the dream traveler. She figured it was probably another patient in an examination room with the door closed. As Erin glanced around their room, Dr. Ruben walked in and quickly greeted Dante with a handshake.

"How are you feeling, Erin? I heard that you had some spotting today? Did it stop?" asked Dr. Ruben.

Erin saw the hurt and surprise on Dante's face, and he said, "What happened? Why didn't you tell me?"

Erin looked at Dante apologetically and said, "Sorry, it just happened this morning, and then I had to go right to an urgent meeting after I called Dr. Ruben's office. Work was crazy this morning, but I'll tell you about that later."

Erin turned her attention to Dr. Ruben and said, "Yes, it was just once this morning, and then it stopped."

Dr. Ruben looked relieved and said, "Good. Did you do anything unusually strenuous in the past day, or did you fall or bump into something?"

Erin was just about to confirm that she fell when she was running from the Terrent last night when she caught herself. Obviously, she wouldn't be able to share that with Dr. Ruben. She paused and then answered, "Only in my dreams."

"All right. Well, please call the office if it happens again."

Erin nodded in agreement.

"OK, let's get to the fun stuff," Dr. Ruben said and smiled as he turned on the ultrasound machine.

Theresa was in the room and prepped Erin for the procedure. Erin unbuttoned her slacks and pulled up her blouse to expose her belly.

Dr. Ruben said, "This will feel a little cold for a second." He applied some clear gel to her abdomen and lightly pressed the ultrasound wand to her belly. Dr. Ruben made some gentle sweeps with the wand and then said, "Well, there we are!"

Erin and Dante looked up at the screen together and saw the magnified, little kidney-bean shadow on the screen.

"Wow!" said Erin. She had known that she was going to be seeing an image of her baby today, but she couldn't have imagined the surge of emotions that it caused. She felt fear and joy at the thought of having a baby, and at the same time, she felt undeniable love for her unborn child. This baby was just a kidney-bean shape, and she did not even know its gender yet, but her love for her unborn baby overwhelmed her. Erin looked at Dante and saw that his eyes had glazed over with tears, and her own tears started. She choked them back just as Theresa adjusted the volume on the machine, and they were able to hear a soft, rapid beating sound.

"We're in luck today! It's not always possible this early, but your baby is in a good position, and that sound is your baby's heartbeat," said Dr. Ruben.

Erin's attempt to hold back her tears failed miserably, and large tears ran down her face, while she wore a silly grin. Theresa knew this type of scenario well, and she subtly passed a tissue in Dante's direction and then handed the box of tissues to Erin. Erin's and Dante's gazes were glued to the image of their baby on the screen. If there had been any doubt over their new baby, it had been obliterated with the sound of its heartbeat. Dante reached out and held Erin's hand, and she gave his hand a quick squeeze back.

Dr. Ruben gave them a minute to enjoy the moment as he took some quick on-screen measurements. "Well, everything looks like it should at this point in your pregnancy. I want to see you again next month, and Theresa will set up that appointment and your next ultrasound appointment before you leave. Do you have any questions for me?"

Erin shook her head no and said, "Thank you, Dr. Ruben."

Theresa helped Erin wipe away the ultrasound gel and sit up on the examination table. Dr. Ruben said, "Please, do call me if you have any more spotting or if you have any questions."

Dante stood up, shook his hand, and said, "Yes, thank you for everything."

Erin and Dante left the office hand-in-hand and decided to have lunch together at a pizzeria across the street. Erin explained everything that had happened at work that day to Dante over lunch.

When Erin paused to sip her water, Dante stated, "I really don't want you working with someone who is that deceptive. Do you still want to keep working at Kaso Pharmaceuticals?"

Erin sighed and responded, "I can't walk away from this study right now. We are so close to finding a cure for pancreatic cancer. I am not going to let Ronan McKenna get to me at this point."

After lunch they parted with a kiss and a hug. As they pulled apart, Dante laid his hand protectively over Erin's abdomen and said, "I know I was not the most receptive to hearing about this pregnancy at first, but I do love you, and I already love this baby we are having."

Erin's eyes welled up again, and she hugged Dante back and said, "Thank you, sweetie. I love you with my whole heart, and I already love this baby too."

Dante smiled and said, "I better get back to the hospital before Dr. Jarvis starts complaining that I left him alone to see all the consults." They parted, and Erin drove back to work.

The rest of Erin's day was quiet compared to her morning. She decided to try to spend the least amount of time thinking of Ronan as possible and just focused on the work she had to do with her study sites. She reviewed data for the rest of the afternoon without a break, and she did not stop until she heard the beep of the text message from Sandra asking to be picked up. Erin left work and went through her normal evening routine of picking up Sandra, grocery shopping, and making and cleaning up dinner. She was exhausted when she finally fell asleep next to Dante, dreaming about what their baby was going to be like.

17

Erin was dreaming about holding a little baby boy. She was holding this baby—who was only a few months old—on her hip, and he was looking at her with his big, innocent bright blue eyes. She was in some type of sports stadium, and there were red stadium seats on both sides of her as she stepped down the cement stairs to go to her seat. She felt the tip of her foot catch air, and her body followed her foot into a falling descent. Erin landed with a thump onto Sienna's green field. The lingering feeling of holding her baby was so pleasant that she wanted to return to the hazy dream. She cleared her head and noticed that she had forgotten to plan an outfit for this visit and was wearing her pajamas.

Erin felt a little silly for forgetting that Sienna would be summoning her tonight to review her first assignment. So much had happened in her daytime world that Erin had completely forgotten about her nighttime world. Erin walked up the curving staircase and stood self-consciously at the top. Sienna smiled when she saw Erin in her pajamas and said, "I see you had a busy day."

Erin hugged Sienna and said, "You will not believe what happened since I last saw you!" They walked over to the garden and settled into the chairs.

"How did you feel about your first assignment last night?" Sienna asked.

Erin paused and then replied, "I kind of felt like a failure when I woke up this morning because I was almost hijacked by a Terrent and needed you to come save me. Plus, I didn't get to observe Jerry Lamar that much."

Sienna said, "Can you tell me exactly what you did observe of Jerry Lamar?"

"I only saw him for about five minutes because his teacher took him inside. As soon as he came outside on the playground, he walked over to the fence and began trying to climb it. His teacher caught him before he made it over and put him in a time-out inside the day care."

"Did you see which direction Jerry was trying to go?" asked Sienna.

"Yes, he was staring directly at me, so I guess he was heading in my direction," answered Erin.

Sienna looked elated and said, "Excellent! I knew it! Erin, you have successfully completed your first assignment because you have identified Jerry Lamar as a Terrent. We call your assignment a Terrent identification visit. Basically, we try to expose possible Terrents to a dream traveler. We do this when they are at a young age so they will not remember or be able to communicate their experience—like when Jerry was a toddler in 1991. We approach them in a controlled environment when their parents are not around. We observe and see how they react. Jerry's mother is a known Terrent, and your work last night confirms that Jerry is also a Terrent. You did a great job!"

Sienna looked content and happy. She sighed and said, "Terrents can naturally sense someone dream traveling within a hundred yard radius around their location, and they become almost obsessed with trying to find the source of their turmoil. They are born with the need to get close to dream travelers in their dream-traveler states. Last night, Jerry was too young to know what to do as a Terrent, but he was determined to get close to your dream-travel presence."

Erin realized that Jerry Lamar was reacting to her sitting near his playground, and his behavior of breaking away from the other children and climbing the fence started to make sense. She considered for a moment, then asked, "Can they control it? I mean, can Terrents control the obsession to get close to dream travelers?"

Sienna looked apprehensive and said, "Yes, but it takes a lot of effort on their part. By the time Terrents reach adulthood, most realize that hijacking dream travelers satisfies their natural obsession and they benefit from being able to travel into the future. Very few Terrents opt to control their natural tendency to hijack a dream traveler."

Erin thought about the way both Jerry and the woman in the parking lot had looked at her. It was almost as if they needed to be near her to survive. Erin shuddered at the thought of being the prey of an obsessed Terrent.

"I can see this topic is making you nervous. Let's talk about something else. The DTC performs three very important functions: preventing Terrent hijacking, Terrent identification, and preventing disasters and tragedies. The first function we discussed at an earlier session when I reviewed all the fluoridation methods that we are employing globally to prevent Terrents from being able to hijack.

"We just discussed the second function of the DTC, and that is to perform Terrent-identification visits like the one you just completed and to manage that information in our database. Thus, the only DTC function that we have not discussed is the role the DTC plays in trying to prevent human disasters and tragedies.

"The Garans perform routine future surveillance to look for future tragedies. Once a tragedy is identified, a strategy is put in place for dream travelers to travel back in time and investigate the elements that may have led to the tragedy. If you receive this type of assignment, the DTC will provide the specific items that will need to be investigated during your assignment."

Erin nodded in understanding.

"You're probably wondering why such bad things are still happening in the world. I know that I would be wondering that."

Erin replied, "That's what I was about to ask you."

Sienna nodded and said, "I know it's unfortunate, but the limited number of Garans prevents us from being able to do as much future surveillance as we need to do. Plus, when the source of a tragedy is in an area populated with Terrents, we're not able to get close enough to the source to effectively understand and prevent the tragedy. The attack on the Twin Towers on September eleventh was an example of how we were not able to collect enough evidence due to Terrent interference. However, we did try to warn the government of the impeding attacks. Some of our past successes do include the prevention of a nuclear war during the Cuban Missile Crisis and multiple airplane crashes that did not occur."

Erin was in awe of this new information and paused thoughtfully before responding. "That is amazing! I can't tell you how proud I am to be part of the DTC. However, it's kind of sad that the DTC has to remain a secret. After all, so much of the DTC's hard work goes unappreciated by society."

Sienna nodded and said, "I know. I feel the same way, but of course we would not be able to function freely if we became public. Could you imagine how governments would try to regulate our activities?"

Erin sighed and said, "Yes, you're right. It would be worse."

"By the way, I jumped right into business matters and forgot to ask about you. How was your day?"

Erin replied, "I had a crazy day. First, I found out that the study director of my team at work was demoted and replaced by a guy that everyone hates. This guy is a kiss-up and should have never been named director because he is completely inexperienced in oncology, and my study is an oncology study. Then, this new guy held an urgent meeting where he insisted on making a lot of unjustified changes that are actually going to jeopardize our study time lines. The worst part is he somehow convinced senior management that these were appropriate changes before he spoke to the study team. Everyone on our study team is scared that he is going to ruin our study!"

Sienna appeared to be absorbing everything Erin was saying. "How can he get away with that?" she asked.

Erin shook her head and said, "I think senior management has no idea what they have unleashed."

"That's a shame," Sienna said.

Erin nodded in agreement and said, "I know, but today was not all bad. I had my first ultrasound this afternoon, and I got to hear the baby's heartbeat!"

Sienna beamed with joy and said, "That is wonderful!"

Erin replied, "Thanks, it was funny because my doctor was trying to figure out why I had spotted this morning, and he asked if I had fallen lately. I almost answered that I had fallen down while being chased by a Terrent! Thankfully, I caught myself and didn't say it, but I did laugh to myself at the time."

Sienna's expression changed, and she said, "You were spotting this morning?"

"Yes, just a little, but then it stopped."

Sienna sighed and looked very disappointed. Erin asked, "What's wrong?"

Sienna paused before saying, "Remember how I told you that you don't have to worry about the injuries you incur when you're dream traveling and about how your scrapes and bruises will disappear when you wake up?"

Erin nodded and said, "Yes, everything was gone when I woke up."

Sienna continued, "Well, we're not sure about how a fetus reacts to injuries incurred during dream travel, and the DTC has been contemplating banning dream travel during pregnancies. I'm not sure if your spotting was related to your fall during dream travel or not. However, I have to report this back to the DTC for further review before I can give you a dream traveler assignment again."

Erin wasn't sure how to feel. She already loved her unborn baby and felt protective of this little being. But she was also torn by her need to carry her share of her dream-traveler responsibility. Erin felt like she was off to a late start by not becoming a dream traveler until her thirties, and she was nervous that there were a lot of other dream travelers who were younger and more experienced than she was. She was aware that pride was a dangerous element in her personality, and she was trying to overcome it, but she didn't want to start out with the handicap of not being able to dream travel like everyone else.

Erin leaned forward in her chair and said, "I really don't think it had anything to do with my fall last night. My doctor reacted like it was fairly common, so maybe it was just a coincidence?"

Sienna still looked concerned and said, "I'm going to put your assignments on hold for now. You did a great job last night, and we really do need help with assignments, but I need to run all of this by the DTC. We can let you know at the meeting."

Erin felt the compliment somewhat soothed the sting that her assignments were going to be placed on hold. "What meeting?" she asked.

Sienna quickly answered, "Oh, sorry, yes, we have the holiday DTC meeting and party on the fourth of January. It will start with a brief meeting and will be followed by our annual holiday party. It's always a lot of fun. All the Garans, and the majority of the dream travelers who are members, will be present. You'll have the chance to meet everyone. We try to accommodate everyone's time zone, so it will start around two o'clock, Eastern Standard Time, on January fourth. That's a Saturday morning, so try to plan to be able to sleep in late that morning to avoid being interrupted."

Erin was excited to finally get the chance to meet other DTs and Garans.

Sienna smiled when she saw Erin's face light up and said, "The meeting and the party will be held at Danny's house, which is on an island near California."

Erin nodded and said, "What should I plan to wear?"

Sienna laughed and said, "Wow, I feel like I have known you so long that I'm forgetting that you haven't been to one of these DTC parties yet. Plan to wear something semiformal. It's not that big of a deal, though, because every year several DTs usually forget and show up in their pajamas. That usually just gets the ball rolling with the jokes and teasing among friends."

Erin smiled but cringed at the thought of meeting the other Garans and DTs for the first time in pajamas, and she made a mental note to put a reminder on her calendar to think about the right type of outfit when going to bed the night before the party. Erin started imagining what the meeting and party would be like.

Sienna said, "I better send you back and let you get some restful sleep."

Erin got up and gave Sienna a hug good-bye. As Sienna stepped back from the hug, she added, "I'm going to let you get some rest in the next few weeks until the party. Please take care of yourself."

Erin nodded and promised that she would as she followed the normal routine of lying down in the lounge chair.

"Wow, I've gotten so used to our visits that I will really miss not seeing you for a few weeks…"

Erin smiled and said, "I know, me too. You know my life is a little hectic, but you can always call me or summon me back just to hang out if you want."

Sienna smiled and said, "I'm going to try and let you rest, but I might have to take you up on that."

Erin smiled back and said, "Anytime." She closed her eyes, and the next time she opened them she was in her dark bedroom lying next to Dante. Erin closed her eyes again and fell back asleep.

18

The next few weeks flew by quickly as Erin wondered what the DTC party would be like. Work was a major distraction because, with Ronan as the study director, Erin's workload had doubled as he delegated more and more of his work to her. Erin's role had always been challenging as the clinical-operations lead under Sarah, but Sarah had always been fair and had pitched in and done her share of the work. However, Ronan pushed every task that came across his desk onto Erin without hesitation.

Ronan had begun calling her at all hours on nights and weekends to ask her questions and for study updates. Whenever he was meeting or going out to dinner with senior management, he would harass Erin for details about the study to appear well prepared and knowledgeable. Erin was growing accustomed to his usual greeting: "Can you do me a favor?"

However, there was not much that Erin could do about it. Erin also knew that she would have to announce her pregnancy sometime in the near future, and she didn't want anyone to complain that she was not fully committed to doing her job because she was pregnant. She was going to have to deal with the additional work and was starting to look forward to her upcoming maternity break in the summer. Erin had read the maternity-leave policy on the company's website several times since she found out she was pregnant, and she knew that she would be able to take off three full months after the birth of her baby. Three months of not having to deal with Ronan McKenna was starting to sound like a luxurious vacation.

Erin was starting to feel very negative about her whole work situation, so she tried to focus on the main reason she loved her job. The work she was doing was important because it gave her the chance to be part of finding a cure for pancreatic cancer. Finding a cure was worth working with a thousand Ronans, and she focused on that thought every time she felt down. On the bright side, Erin had been essentially healthy and had not had any bleeding episodes since the first one.

Christmas day was hectic. The celebration started at Dante's parents' house. Next Dante and Erin dropped off Sandra at her mother's house, and then they continued to David's house to spend time with Erin's parents and family. Erin and Dante decided to celebrate New Year's Eve at home, and they sipped nonalcoholic champagne as they watched the ball drop in New York City on TV.

Weeks had flown by, and it was finally the day before the DTC meeting and holiday party. Erin was extremely excited about going to her first DTC gathering. Erin had always felt that she was different from most people, and for the first time in her life, she understood why. She enjoyed knowing that there were other people just like her. Erin had spent the first half of her life completely oblivious to the dream-travel world, and she finally felt complete.

On the evening of January the third, Erin could barely contain herself. She had found a navy-blue cocktail dress in a catalog that she thought would be perfect for the occasion. Dante had called at eight o'clock to say that he had three more patients to see at the hospital and that he would not be home for at least another two hours. Erin said good night to Sandra at nine o'clock and started getting ready for bed. By half past nine, Erin was tucked away in bed and was visualizing herself wearing the outfit she had chosen when she fell into a deep sleep.

19

Erin dreamed that she and Dante were going to the mailbox to look for an envelope that Dante was expecting to receive in the mail. Oddly, they were walking on a narrow wooden walkway when Erin slipped off. She reached for Dante, but she could not grab him before she felt the bump as she landed on both feet on a firm surface. She immediately shaded her eyes with her hand because it was so bright that she was temporarily blinded by the sunlight.

As Erin gradually regained her vision, she realized she had been summoned to a new place. Still shading her eyes with her hands, she saw that she was standing in the center of a courtyard. Spanish Mission Style terra-cotta tiles stretched out to cover a very large enclosed courtyard that seemed like it reached at least an acre in each direction. The courtyard was enclosed on three sides by the walls of a sprawling, large building. A sand-colored stucco wall that was at least fifteen feet high enclosed the fourth side. Large palm trees were planted throughout the courtyard, providing some shade, and off to the side, a ten-foot-high fountain with three basin-type tiers provided a tranquil sound as the water spilled down each level.

As Erin turned around to examine her surroundings, she saw a group of about thirty people under a tent in the corner. They were sitting in rows of chairs facing a table that was on a small, raised stage. Sienna sat in the center of the table, beckoning Erin toward her. Erin felt a wave of relief to see a familiar face and walked toward the tent. As she approached, she noticed Sienna was sitting with five other people, and Erin realized that they must be the other Garans.

A petite Filipino woman sat on Sienna's right. Erin knew that she must be Rayna, the woman who raised Sienna. Rayna had shoulder-length, silky black hair, and her bangs were cut very short to frame her kind-looking face. Erin guessed that Rayna must be at least fifty years old, but she had an almost childish appearance that made her seem much younger. Erin assumed that Sienna must have told Rayna about her because Rayna smiled and waved in such a welcoming way that Erin's fear of meeting the other Garans vanished.

Erin entered the tent and began walking down the center aisle, between rows of chairs. The other four people at the front table turned their attention to Erin all at the same time. A soft, warm breeze blew her hair back, and she felt surprisingly comfortable and confident. Now the people who were sitting in the rows of chairs facing the table had turned their heads in her direction. The dream travelers appear to range in age from young tweens and teenagers to several elderly individuals. They were diverse and appeared to come from all over the globe. Several people in the audience were wearing black headsets.

Sienna stood up from her chair, quickly scooted around the table, stepped down the two steps of the stage, and walked to greet Erin with a big smile and a hug.

"I missed you, and I'm so happy you are here!" They walked together toward the Garan table. By then, most of the other Garans were filing down the steps toward them. Sienna started the introductions right away. First she waved her hand in the direction of the petite Filipino woman and said, "Erin, this is my second mother and good friend Rayna Diwa!"

Rayna reached out her small, delicate hand and shook Erin's hand gently. She said, "It is a pleasure to meet you, Erin."

Erin replied, "It's a pleasure to meet you also."

In quick succession Sienna pointed to the other members of the small half circle that had surrounded them. "This is Quinn Walsh," she said, pointing to a tall, fair-skinned, middle-aged gentleman with cropped black hair. Quinn had a medium build and was at least six feet three inches tall. He had rosy cheeks, a few days' worth of beard stubble, and an extremely dominant chin. As she reached forward to shake his hand, she saw that Quinn's left eye was blue, but his right eye was green. Erin tried not to stare, but it was the first time she had met someone with two different eye colors. In a sweet-sounding Irish brogue, Quinn replied, "It is a pleasure to meet you, Erin."

Erin shook Quinn's hand and replied, "It's a pleasure to meet you."

Next Sienna pointed to a tall adolescent Asian man with short, black, spiky hair and said, "This is Takumi Ito."

Takumi quickly nodded and bowed his head and said hello in a heavily accented voice. From his accent Erin guessed he was probably from Japan. Takumi had blushed and backed away as he was introduced. She assumed he was shy and refrained from shaking his hand and nodded her head in return and said, "Nice to meet you."

Takumi smiled in relief and continued to slightly bow and nod his head. He had a friendly smile, but the front teeth that appeared too big for his mouth and the scattered acne on his face seemed to indicate that he was hovering between adolescence and adulthood. Erin guessed he was around twenty years old.

Sienna pointed to a man with a thick build and suntanned skin who was a few inches taller than Erin and said, "This is Danny Taylor, and we are actually at his house right now."

Danny had short, sandy-blond, uncombed hair and looked about the same age as Erin. He smiled and said, "Hey, nice to meet you, and welcome to Santa Catalina Island."

Erin replied, "It is nice to meet you, too." She leaned forward, shook Danny's hand, and said, "Where is this island located?"

Danny replied, "It's right off the coast of California. I live here with Jaja." He pointed over his shoulder to the elderly man who had remained alone at the table.

Sienna turned toward the table and said, "Yes, this is Jaja Eze; he is from Nigeria, but he currently lives here with Danny."

Jaja had dark black skin and snow-white, short hair. He was sitting hunched over and appeared extremely old and tired. He had a friendly smile, and he attempted to speak with a scratchy, gruff voice before coughing for a moment and then clearing his throat. He finally spoke, with a light Nigerian accent, in a gentle voice that was almost a whisper. "A pleasure to meet you, Erin."

Erin walked to the table and gently shook Jaja's fragile, bony hand. She replied, "It is very nice to meet you also, Mr. Eze." Erin could tell that Jaja commanded respect and felt it would be disrespectful to call him by his first name.

However, Jaja Eze replied, "Please call me Jaja."

Erin nodded. She already liked Jaja. It was hard not to like a man who smiled as if they were all his own grandchildren. She noted that Jaja was indeed frail. Even though it was at least eighty degrees outside, he was wearing black wool pants and a thick brown sweater. He also had a blanket draped over his shoulders. Erin guessed that Jaja must be at least ninety years old.

Sienna put her arm in Erin's arm and turned toward the rows of chairs. Sienna cleared her throat and said, "I would like to introduce our newest dream traveler, Erin Brusca."

The audience was composed of about thirty people or so, and most were smiling and lightly clapping in response to the introduction. All were looking at Erin with their full attention. Erin felt a little self-conscious. She was a delayed dream traveler and wondered if that made her appear silly to those who discovered their dream-traveler gift during puberty. Sienna waved her hand toward the rows of chairs and said, "Please have a seat."

As Erin glanced at the rows of chairs, she made eye contact with Steve. He immediately waved and smiled at Erin. No seats were available near Steve, so Erin sat on an empty chair in the first row, next to a woman in her sixties who wore her whitish-gray hair cut short in an almost military-style, buzz haircut. Erin smiled warmly at her as she sat down, but the woman ignored Erin and turned the other way. The woman had dark-brown eyes with equally dark circles under her eyes. The combination gave the woman an almost hound-dog-like appearance. Erin was a little surprised by the cold response.

She looked up as Sienna said, "We are just waiting on one more—"

Before Sienna could finish her sentence, a male voice from outside the tent yelled, "*Oh man, not again!*"

Erin was nervous at first, but the rest of the group began to break out in giggles and stifled laughs. Erin looked toward the entrance of the tent and saw the source of everyone's laughter. A middle-aged man was wearing his red, polka-dot boxer shorts and nothing else. He had disheveled, gray, wiry hair, and wore wire-rimmed glasses with thick lenses that made his brown eyes appear enormous. He was trying to hide his lack of clothing by hunching over and sort of shading himself with his hands.

While everyone else was smiling, the cold woman next to Erin muttered, "Ridiculous. That Ted is such an embarrassment…"

Erin ignored the grumpy woman and couldn't help smiling at seeing someone do exactly what Erin had been afraid she was going to do: forget to think about an outfit before falling asleep. Danny grabbed a folded white robe from a table in the corner and walked toward Ted, smiling. Erin guessed that an emergency supply of robes must come in handy at events such as these. Ted gratefully accepted the robe from Danny, wrapped it around himself, and then gave Danny a half hug and pat on the back.

In a booming voice, Ted explained to the entire group, "I was all prepared for tonight, with an outfit in mind, when my wife started in on me before we went to bed. She said that I was insensitive because I didn't notice her haircut! Can you believe that? What is wrong with that woman? I told her that she never notices when I get my hair cut. There was even that time when I shaved my mustache, and she kissed me good-bye that morning and didn't notice I had shaved until dinner that night when my son pointed it out!"

Ted finished his story and scanned the group, seeking consensus. He passed his gaze over Erin and then quickly returned. "Hey, I didn't know we had a new member." He started to walk toward Erin with his hand out, ready to shake hands. Unfortunately, he had not done a good job of tying his robe, and the cord was dragging in front of him. Erin was about to warn him when the tie caught under Ted's foot, and he tripped and landed at Erin's feet. The whole group broke into a new chorus of giggles. Ted blushed as he stood up, but he also looked like he enjoyed being the clown of the group. He tied his robe correctly, held out his hand, and said, "Let's try this again. I'm Ted Roth."

Erin shook his hand and replied, "Hello, Ted. I'm Erin Brusca."

Sienna called the group to order by saying, "OK, I guess we better get started." Ted took a seat in the first row, and Sienna went back up to the table in the front and sat down.

Rayna stepped down from the small stage and said, "Welcome, everyone!" The crowd responded with a soft round of clapping. "As everyone now knows, we have a new member joining us, Erin Brusca." This announcement was followed by another soft round of applause from everyone except the grumpy woman next to Erin, who just rolled her eyes. Erin was not sure what she had done to upset this woman, but she was too distracted to put too much time into figuring it out.

Rayna's expression became more serious, and she said, "I will try to cover all the business items quickly so we can move on to the holiday celebration. First, thank you everyone for updating your member profiles online. Please make sure your e-mail and contact information are always kept up-to-date to ensure we are able to reach you as needed. Next, we have released the newest version of the Terrent Locator program on our website." Rayna went on to present several slides that explained how to log into the new system and navigate through the website.

"Please be sure that you check the website before all dream travel, both assigned and leisure travel." Erin was surprised that DTs were allowed to dream travel at their leisure. She had many questions about that, but she didn't want to interrupt the meeting with all her new-member questions. "Are there any questions on the newest version?" Rayna asked. "It's pretty self-explanatory."

Rayna continued, "OK, I also want to alert everyone that the Terrents have been heard whispering about some kind of prophecy recently. This prophecy predicts that during the first tetrad of this century, the most powerful Garan will be born to a Terrent. As you may know, a tetrad is a series of four consecutive total lunar eclipses. If you remember the first total lunar eclipse of this tetrad took place last year on May sixteenth and the last of the four total lunar eclipses will be on October twenty-eigth. We have done some brief investigating, and we have not seen any signs that this powerful Garan has been born, but please report back if you see or hear anything that might be relevant. Of course we will do everything possible to ensure that the Garan protocol is followed and that this infant Garan will be found and protected at one of our Garan residences."

Rayna paused before continuing. "The last item I want to cover during the meeting is the issue of dream travel during pregnancy. I know this has come up before, but the DTC has finally outlined some basic guidelines about how to approach this issue. From this point forward, all dream-travel assignments will be halted from the time the pregnancy is identified until the dream traveler delivers the baby. The DTC recognizes that the best chance we have of increasing our DT numbers is through own members having children. Thus, we must take a conservative approach and protect every DT pregnancy from any potential danger." There were several nods in acknowledgment of this new guideline.

Erin's heart sunk. She didn't realize how much she had looked forward to dream traveling again until she heard she would not be able to travel for several months. As Rayna continued on with a few more announcements, Erin wondered if she would be able to learn more about dream travel and, perhaps, practice her technique with Sienna until she could travel on her own again.

"Does anyone else have any other business to discuss?" Rayna asked. The group remained silent, so Rayna concluded. "Since there is nothing else to discuss, this meeting is adjourned. Please leave your translation headsets on your chairs, and everyone is welcome to join us in the courtyard for the celebration!"

Erin heard pop music start to play outside the tent, and everyone stood up and began to socialize. Sienna, Rayna, and Ted came up to Erin at the same time and all started talking at once.

They paused, and Sienna said, "Erin, are you OK with the new pregnancy guideline? I am sorry that it all happened like this, but once the baby is born, I am sure we will keep you busy with tons of assignments."

Erin nodded at the same time that Ted smiled and asked, "You're pregnant? Well congratulations are in order! That is great that we have another reason to celebrate!" Ted looked like a mad scientist, but he had such a goofy, yet sincere, nature that Erin couldn't help liking him instantly.

Rayna smiled and said, "Yes, we are very happy to have Erin as our newest member, and we're excited about the potential for another new dream traveler to be born in the near future!"

Rayna and Ted wandered away and began talking about a new book that Ted had just read. Sienna took Erin by the arm and said, "Let me introduce you to everyone and show you around."

As they exited the tent together, Erin noticed the grumpy woman standing by herself in the corner of the tent and whispered to Sienna, "Who is that woman? She was kind of rude to me, and she seems to be very unpleasant in general."

Sienna replied, "That's Agnes. Try not to pay too much attention to her. She lost her husband last year in a freak accident. He was killed when a taxi in New York City jumped the curb and pinned him against a building."

Erin felt guilty for speaking negatively about Agnes when she had experienced such a horrible loss. She couldn't imagine her own life without Dante. Sienna continued, "It was very sad because Agnes's husband had just retired a few weeks earlier, and they were on their way to enjoy a Broadway show together. At a time in her life when she was just about to start enjoying retirement, he was taken away from her."

Sienna paused and then said, "Agnes came to the DTC and asked permission to dream travel back to that night and prevent her husband's death. She pleaded so intensely, but sadly, we had to deny her request."

Erin felt her first disenchantment with the DTC. "Why would the DTC deny her?"

"We did an investigation, and we had to deny her request due to future circumstances. Unfortunately, I am not allowed to explain that further, but all of us wished we had been able to grant her request. She has not been the same since. She has only attended the mandatory meetings and will probably not be joining us for the celebration."

Erin's mother had always told her not to judge people because it was impossible to know what they are dealing with in their own lives. Erin took one more glance at Agnes and regretted stereotyping her as grouchy.

Sienna continued to guide Erin into the open area of the courtyard. During the meeting, two round tables with evergreen trimming had been set up, and a DJ was playing music in the corner by the back wall of the courtyard. Erin saw that Danny was pushing Jaja in a wheelchair toward that section and that most of the group had gathered around the two tables.

As Erin and Sienna approached the rest of the group, Sienna said, "One thing I haven't talked about yet is that you really should not eat or drink when you dream travel. You can do it, but it will typically cause you to have an upset stomach when you wake up. What we usually do instead is enjoy the sensation created by cinnamon."

Erin was intrigued and said, "I don't understand."

"I'm sorry. That probably didn't make much sense to you. I forgot to explain that, for some reason, cinnamon has a very unusual side effect during dream travel. It gives a dream traveler an almost euphoric sensation. We can smell cinnamon-scented items, or we can enjoy it as flavored gum, lozenges, and candy, without experiencing the upset stomach we would get by consuming food or beverages."

Erin nodded as she absorbed this new information. As they got closer to the group, Erin saw red candles burning on the tables and smelled their cinnamon scent. Sienna reached the first table, picked up a stick of gum, and handed it to Erin. Erin saw that some of the others were chewing gum, some were licking red lollipops, and some had started to dance in the area of the courtyard in front of the DJ.

Erin unwrapped the cinnamon-flavored gum and popped it in her mouth. An instantaneous warmth washed over her body, and she felt flushed from her head down to her toes. A feeling of bliss replaced her fears and inhibitions. She heard the repetitive sound of the bass beating within every cell of her body, and she felt almost at one with the song being played.

Almost everyone was dancing and swaying at this point, and she joined in on the fun. Everyone had glazed eyes and a slightly drunken look, and each song played seemed better than the last. Erin didn't want the dancing to ever end.

She was dancing next to Sienna when someone took her hand and turned her in a gentle spin. She saw that it was the Garan Quinn spinning her, and she had to tilt her head all the way back to look at him. Quinn's eyes looked glazed, and he smiled and said, "So how did we lose you to the other side?"

Erin was caught off guard and stopped dancing. "Excuse me?"

Quinn chuckled and said, "I saw your profile. You were born Erin McGowan of full Irish descent, and you married an Italian. I have to call you a traitor."

Erin had been teased and called a traitor by other Irish American friends, and she laughed at the remark as she resumed dancing. "I couldn't resist the Italian food."

Quinn laughed in return and gently spun her one more time.

Erin liked the sweet sound of Quinn's brogue, and her flirtatious smile was a reflexive action. He returned her smile, and Erin realized that she was actually attracted to this sweet-talking man with different-colored eyes and gentle dance moves. She quickly remembered that she was a happily married woman and felt a little guilty at her actions. Erin politely said, "Well, thank you for the dance." Then she excused herself from the dance floor. She preoccupied herself with looking at the table of cinnamon-flavored gums and candies. She contemplated trying a cinnamon-flavored lollipop.

Rayna joined Erin at the table and said, "Are you having a good time?"

Erin smiled and happily said, "Yes, everything is wonderful."

Rayna continued, "I hope you understand why we have the new pregnancy guidelines. Sienna was afraid that you would be upset, but we have to be conservative on behalf of your baby."

Erin nodded and said, "I know. I was a little upset, but it's because I want to be a team player and help out."

Rayna replied, "We appreciate that and will definitely keep you busy in the future. I spoke to Sienna, and since she isn't training anyone else right now, she's going to summon you to her place once a week and do some informal training sessions with you. Informal training sessions are something new, but since there is so much to learn, I would prefer that you continue to get exposed to as much as possible about the dream-traveler world in a safe setting like Sienna's home."

Erin loved spending time with Sienna and answered, "I would like that very much."

Sienna saw Rayna and Erin talking and stopped dancing to join them at the table. Rayna said, "Well, it looks like we are all set to have a few months of informal training sessions for Erin at your place, Sienna."

Sienna replied, "Perfect. I hate to be the first to end the fun tonight, but, Erin, I better get you back home soon. It's approaching sunrise on the East Coast."

Erin was shocked at how quickly the evening had gone by, and she nodded in agreement. "Thank you for having me here. It was nice to meet everyone, and I had a great time dancing."

Rayna gave Erin a hug good-bye, and Sienna and Erin began walking toward the back wall of Danny's home, where several lounge chairs were lined up under a palm tree. Erin knew the routine by now. She hugged Sienna good-bye, lay down on the nearest lounge chair, and began to close her eyes.

Sienna said, "Oh, before I forget, we will have our sessions weekly on Friday nights, if that's OK with you."

Erin replied, "That sounds perfect. I will see you next Friday."

She closed her eyes briefly, and when she opened them again, she was next to Dante in bed. The room was already lit with the morning sun peeking through the sides of the window blinds. Erin closed her eyes again and fell back asleep, reliving the beat of the dance music and the euphoric happiness of cinnamon.

20

The rest of Erin's weekend flew by. Before she knew it, it was Monday morning, and she was back at work, sitting in front of her computer, sipping coffee, and going through her e-mail messages. Erin saw an e-mail invitation from Ronan requesting a meeting with Erin at nine o'clock that morning. Erin wondered why Ronan was requesting that she meet with him alone in his office, and she became nervous as she worried that he was taking her aside to reprimand her. Erin quickly searched her mind, but she could not figure out Ronan's motivation. She gave up trying and accepted that she would find out very soon.

Erin completed reviewing and answering her e-mails just in time to gather her notebook, coffee, and BlackBerry and walk over to Ronan's office. His door was closed, but as soon as she knocked, she heard him say, "Come in." Erin was surprised to see Ronan looking so pleasant and friendly. He smiled and gestured to the chairs in front of his desk. "Please have a seat," he said. Erin gently closed the office door behind her and sat down in one of the two chairs in front of Ronan's desk.

"First, I want to thank you for accepting this meeting invitation on such short notice," Ronan began. Erin was on her guard and just politely nodded in response. Ronan continued, "I also want to apologize for possibly getting off on the wrong foot with you. The last few weeks have been very chaotic, and I have not been myself. I was in such a hurry to manage this study that I did not get the chance to get to know the members of my team. So I hope you can accept my apology."

Erin was taken aback by this uncharacteristic behavior, but she tried for an understanding expression and said, "No worries. It's understandable with all the responsibility you have taken on."

Ronan shocked Erin further by replying, "No, it's not OK. My behavior has been embarrassing, and I plan to make it up to you and the rest of the team. I would like to see if everyone is available to go to eat out at Petra's for lunch today. It would be my pleasure to treat the whole team to a well-deserved, nice meal."

Erin knew that Petra's Restaurant was the most expensive restaurant in town and that Ronan's gesture was going to cost several hundred dollars. She was confused by his generous offer, but she could only answer, "I will e-mail everyone to see if today is good and let you know." She stumbled through her thank you and left Ronan's office to start the procedure of checking everyone's schedule to see who was free to go.

Erin started receiving phone calls in response to her e-mail right away. She was asked the same question several times: Why is Ronan offering to take everyone to lunch? In response, Erin tried to relay his message about how he felt badly about the way he had treated everyone and wanted to make amends. Everyone agreed to meet at the restaurant at noon.

Erin and Molly decided to ride together in Erin's car, and they hypothesized the whole way to the restaurant. Molly did not trust her brother-in-law and could not figure out what was motivating him. As they pulled into Petra's parking lot, they saw Greg Chan, the study biostatistician, and Jenny Choo, the study database programmer, walking through the parking lot. Greg was a slight, Asian man in his midfifties, with round cheeks and thinning silver hair. Jenny Choo was an extremely thin, shy Chinese American with tiny facial features and black hair cut in a page-boy haircut. They approached the front door, but they looked hesitant as they entered the building.

When Erin and Molly went inside, it took Erin's eyes a second to adjust to the dim lighting, but she soon noticed that the restaurant was beautiful. The walls were dark wood with elegant crown molding. There was royal-red-and-navy patterned velvet fabric draped from ceiling to floor, dressing the windows and doorways. The chairs had ornate wood backings and were thickly upholstered in a matching regal fabric. Centered in front of the double-door entry was an elegant room with a twenty-foot-long mahogany bar. The dark wood of the bar was so polished that its surface glowed like obsidian in the dim light.

Erin and Molly saw that they were the last to arrive. The rest of the team was already lined up at the bar, sipping various drinks. Ronan was standing in the center of the group, and he smiled when he saw Erin and Molly enter.

A silver-haired waiter, dressed in a black tuxedo and holding a tray of hors d'oeuvres, walked over to Molly, Erin, and Brenda Collins, the study's data manager. As he offered the little pastries to them, he handed them napkins and asked, "Would you like a drink?"

Erin knew that people would question her if she didn't order something, so she said, "Red wine, please." Molly asked for the same.

Most of the group seemed to have arrived early. They looked like they were feeling the effects of the alcohol because they were giggling and acting chummy with Ronan. Ronan was smiling from ear to ear and was making his way through the crowd, joking with team members as he went.

Erin turned to Brenda and asked, "Did everyone get here early?"

Brenda was in her midforties. She had pale skin, blue eyes, and straw-colored hair that was always pulled into a tight bun on the back of her head. She was shorter than Erin and slightly overweight. She was holding a cosmopolitan in her hand and quickly answered, "Ronan saw most of us leaving an eleven o'clock meeting and suggested that we carpool and come over early. You know, I wasn't sure about him, but he really does seem to be a good guy."

Ronan made his way over to them. He rested his hand on Erin's shoulder and said, "Thank you for setting this up, Erin." Erin was surprised that he thanked her for something as simple as an e-mail invite after she had worked for so many weeks without him offering a word of gratitude. She was not used to this "new" Ronan, and something felt off. The waiter returned with two glasses of wine. Molly took a sip, and Erin pretended to as well.

Ronan began, "Now that everyone is here, I would like to propose a toast." The rest of the group raised their drinks in the air. Ronan continued, "I would like to thank all of you for your hard work on this team and toast to new beginnings! May we have a successful outcome to this very important study!" Everyone clinked glasses together and responded with a hearty, "Cheers!"

Ronan patted Molly on the back, smiled, and said, "How is my sister-in-law doing? You know your sister's birthday is coming up, and I want to get her something special. Would you mind going with me to the jeweler some time this week to help me pick out something really nice? Of course I'll throw something in for you too for helping me."

Molly looked surprised and could only respond, "Sure."

"Perfect," Ronan responded. "And thanks." He made his way back to the rest of the group, where he was greeted with smiles.

As Molly and Brenda began talking about electronic case-report forms, Erin pretended to be interested in a painting of a horse that was hanging near a corner of the room. She slowly made her way over to it, looked around quickly to make sure no one was watching, and poured more than half of her wine in the potted plant in the corner of the room. Erin returned to Brenda and Molly just as the hostess was leading everyone into the dining room.

Erin sat between Brenda and Molly at the large table that had been set up for their team. The rest of their lunch was similar to their time in the bar. Everyone smiled, laughed, and occasionally mentioned that they had never realized that Ronan was such a nice guy. Erin thought the food was exquisite.

At the end of the meal, Ronan quietly handed the waiter his credit card, and Erin began to question her skepticism. Maybe Ronan was truly a changed man. As they prepared to leave the restaurant, Ronan excused everyone from work for the rest of the afternoon and said they could go home early. Erin dropped off Molly at her car and drove home, thinking that everyone was entitled to a second chance, including Ronan.

21

The rest of Erin's week was fairly uneventful. She arrived at work early on Friday and tried to get a jump-start on her day. Erin needed to catch up after a full week of nonstop interruptions at the office. Ever since the lunch on Monday, people from all different departments kept stopping by and saying things like, "You know, I have known Ronan for two years, and I have never seen this side of him" or, "I wonder what Ronan would say about how to fix the enrollment problem they are having on John Harold's study?" Erin cherished the peaceful quietness of the office when she arrived at half past seven, a hour before most people started their day.

As Erin started her normal routine of reviewing e-mails and following up on ongoing study issues, she noticed that the first e-mail was from S.Goodman@dmail.com. Erin smiled, knowing that it was an e-mail from Sienna. She clicked on Sienna's e-mail and saw the message:

Dearest Erin,
I am so sorry to cancel on you like this, but I have good news. We have another new dream traveler! She is only twelve years old, so I am fully dedicating the next three weeks to her training. I am sorry I will not be able to meet with you as scheduled, but Quinn has volunteered to take over our weekly lessons until I am freed up again. I have briefed him on what we have already covered, and he is ready to pick up

where I left off. He will be summoning you tonight at the same time, so
please remember to go to bed early. Also, dress warmly because the aver-
age temperature in Ireland at this time of year is about forty degrees
Fahrenheit.
Warmest regards,
Sienna

Erin didn't know how to feel about the e-mail. She was happy that
a new dream traveler truly was a celebrated event; the knowledge
helped her feel assured that the DTC's warm welcome at the party
was sincere. However, she had been looking forward to spending
time with Sienna. Since Erin could not talk to anyone else about being a dream traveler—at least, no one who believed her—she needed
sessions with Sienna just to be able to talk freely with at least one
person. Plus, Erin was a little embarrassed to see Quinn again. At
the DTC holiday party, the effect of the cinnamon had caused Erin
to feel drunk and to act a little flirtier than she should have. She was
hoping she hadn't come across as silly or pathetic to Quinn.

Erin decided that she would remain professional during these
sessions with Quinn and tried to push the e-mail and her appointment with Quinn out of her head and get some work done. Erin had a
heap of reports and paperwork that she had to review, so she worked
all morning and ate lunch at her desk.

Erin was deep in thought as she read a new guideline on obtain-
ing informed consent from non-English-speaking patients when
someone behind her cleared her throat. Erin gasped, as she always
seemed to do when someone startled her, and then laughed at herself
when she saw Molly standing behind her.

"Hey, I haven't seen you all day," Molly began.

Erin answered, "I know. I didn't get a lot of work done this week,
so I locked myself away today to try and catch up."

"Oh, I see. Any good plans this weekend?" Molly asked.

Erin almost laughed again when she thought how farfetched it
would sound if she told Molly that she was going to be summoned

by a Garan named Quinn to his home on an island off the coast of Ireland tonight to continue her dream-traveler lessons. Erin contained her smile and responded, "Not too many. Dante is on call, so we can't really do too much."

Molly smiled from ear to ear and responded, "Ronan just put together a ski trip and invited Jack, me, and my whole family to go with my sister, Kerry, and him to some resort in Vermont." Molly was practically bubbling over with excitement, and Erin was pleased for her.

Erin's cell phone chimed, and she grabbed it from her purse and saw that she had a text message from Sandra.

Molly quickly said, "I better get going. Have a great weekend!"

Erin responded, "Yes, you too! I can't wait to hear the details on Monday!" As Molly walked away, Erin's cell phone rang.

As soon as Erin pressed answer, she heard Sandra's voice say, "I went to Nicole's house after school. Is it OK if I sleep over here tonight?"

Erin responded, "Yes. I will let your father know."

As Erin pressed End on her phone, she noticed that it was already half past five. She packed up her stuff, got in the car, and drove home.

The house was empty when Erin arrived, and she automatically hit the Play button on the answering machine when she saw the flashing red light. Erin heard Dante's voice say, "Hey, sweetie, I hate being on call. It's five o'clock, and I still have six critical-care consults to see! I probably won't be home until after ten, so don't wait up for me. I'll grab something for dinner from the cafeteria. Love you."

Erin realized it had been a long time since she had a night alone to herself and decided she would celebrate her bachelorette night by eating junk food and watching a romantic movie by herself.

She changed into her pajamas, grabbed a bag of Cheez Doodles and the remote control, and settled into the couch. The movie started with a panorama of a snowy mountainside, and she reminded herself that she needed a warm outfit for her session tonight. She started thinking about her visit with Quinn, and she couldn't focus on the movie. What was his home like? Where would she land when she was summoned? Erin wished that she could just go to Sienna's home.

The movie was over by nine o'clock, so Erin brushed her teeth, washed her face, and lay down in bed. She was tired from a long week and felt sort of lonely in bed by herself. In the midst of feeling sorry for herself, she remembered that she had to think of an outfit for her session tonight. She started scanning her mind for something to wear. She thought about her blue sweater, but considered its plunging neckline and decided that might not be the look she was going for. She decided on something safe; a black turtleneck, blue jeans, her black boots, and her black wool coat would be perfect.

Erin envisioned herself in that outfit and let her body relax in bed. She felt all her muscles let go of the day's fatigue, and she slowed her breathing into a soothing pattern. Her last thought was of the final scene of the movie she had watched that evening. The female lead was relaxing on a beautiful Caribbean beach. It would be great, she thought, to get away and take a nice Caribbean vacation.

Erin felt herself land gently on a soft, moist surface, and upon opening her eyes, she saw that she was sitting in some type of peat moss. There was a freezing-cold breeze, and she smelled the dampness of the ocean. She was already shivering and realized that she had made a huge mistake. When she looked down, she saw she was only wearing the blue bikini the female lead of the movie had worn.

"I am an idiot!" Erin muttered out loud. Erin saw that the sky was overcast, and there was a large stone wall on her left. The only opening in the wall was a giant iron gate, about one hundred feet away. Off to the right, about a quarter of a mile away, Erin thought she saw the ocean, but it was hard to tell through the thick fog.

The cold had hit Erin's body hard, and her violent shivering was becoming almost painful. As she stood up with her arms hugging herself, she saw a tall man in a black jacket running toward her. If Erin hadn't been so cold, she would have been embarrassed. As it was, she could only be relieved when she realized it was Quinn approaching.

"Hang on; I'll have you inside in a moment." In one quick motion, he whipped his long, black wool jacket off, wrapped it around her, and swept her up so that he was carrying her like a baby.

Erin could barely see because the warm jacket was almost covering her face. As Quinn quickly carried her through the gates and toward the front of the building, Erin saw what looked like a giant stone castle. As they entered, Erin took a deep breath and smelled a sweet scent that was a hint of cologne blended with Quinn's natural manly scent. Between the warmth of the jacket and the sweet smell of Quinn, Erin was feeling disoriented by the time Quinn gently placed her down to stand in front of the fire that was burning in the huge stone fireplace. He had carried her into a living room beautifully decorated in medieval style with ancient-looking paintings of people from the past hanging on the walls.

Quinn spoke in his husky Irish accent. "You Americans really like to make an entrance! Don't get me wrong—I love the view—but you may want to hold off until warmer weather to show off that lovely body of yours, Erin. I can't have you catching pneumonia after our first session!"

Erin blushed from head to foot, thinking how stupid she must look showing up in a bikini in the winter in Ireland. Her teeth were chattering together as she shivered and said, "I wasss…was…thinking of something…thing else…but…but…thought…of this by accident."

Quinn gently wrapped his jacket more tightly around her and rubbed her arms. "Shhh, it's OK. Hang on; I'll be right back."

Quinn returned a minute later with two mugs filled with steaming liquid. He handed one mug to Erin and began sipping the other. "Go ahead. It will warm you up," Quinn said as he sipped his drink.

Erin brought the mug to her lips and tasted a sweet blend of warm juice. She took a short sip, followed by a large gulp, and felt the warmth of the drink permeate her body. She instantly felt warmer—to the point that she was almost sweating. She pulled away from the drink, remembering the euphoric feeling from the cinnamon at the DTC party. This warm juice had cinnamon in it, Erin was sure, and she had the same feeling but even more strongly. "Wait, does this have alcohol in it?" Erin asked.

Quinn nodded.

Erin explained, "Oh, thank you, but I can't drink this. I'm pregnant."

Quinn must have been feeling the effects of the cinnamon because his eyes were glazed over and he had a sensual look of hunger on his face when he said, "You would never know it. You look great in that bikini!"

Erin blushed, and although she was too warm, she kept Quinn's jacket tightly wrapped around her. "I am so sorry for showing up like this," said Erin. "It was a mistake. A movie with a tropical scene had me longing for a beach vacation…Could I bother you for something other than your coat to wear?"

Quinn regained his composure and apologized as he rushed out of the room and returned seconds later with a navy-blue satin robe. "Here you go," Quinn said in an apologetic tone as he passed the robe to Erin. She quickly removed the heavy coat and replaced it with the robe. As she tied the robe around herself, Quinn looked like he was torn between disappointment and relief. He shook his head and pointed to the large, brown leather sofa and said, "Please, sit down."

Erin was feeling the full effects of the cinnamon by that point and couldn't help smiling. She felt silly for looking so happy, but the cinnamon had that effect, and she wanted to dance. She tried to compose herself as she looked at Quinn sitting in the armchair opposite her. He was wearing a white dress shirt with the sleeves rolled up past his elbows and dark-blue jeans. His fitted shirt made it obvious that Quinn had a muscular frame and large shoulders. He was leaning back in the chair with his left ankle crossed over his right knee, and he was wearing an equally content smile, his eyes twinkling in the dim lighting. Erin had to admit that Quinn was extremely attractive and that she was having a hard time focusing on the fact that she was there to learn. Her mind kept running loose, wondering if he had six-pack abs under that shirt.

Quinn interrupted her train of thought by saying, "I am sorry about the drink having rum. I should have known better because I felt the baby's energy when I summoned you."

Erin snapped out of her daydream with the reminder that she was pregnant. She answered, "Yes, Sienna said the same thing about feeling the energy of the baby."

Quinn stated, "You know that you're definitely having a dream traveler, right? I mean, Garans can't feel regular human energy or even Terrent energy. Garans only feel the energy of those with the ability to dream travel."

Erin tried to grasp the fact and said, "No, I didn't realize that. Sienna didn't mention it to me." Erin's felt disturbed that her child would have the same ability to dream travel as she did. She never wanted her unborn baby to have to run from a Terrent.

Quinn continued as if he could read her mind, "Don't worry. We will cross that bridge when we come to it. For now we should focus on your training."

Erin nodded in agreement, but she vowed to herself that she was not going to let anyone hurt her baby. She was still amazed at how protective she became over this unborn child she hadn't met yet. She hadn't even felt the baby move, and she already felt more protective of it than she did for any other human.

Quinn began, "I did a little research on you, Erin. Was your paternal grandmother Margaret Donnelly from county Roscommon in Ireland?"

"Yes!" Erin answered.

"I thought so. My paternal grandfather lived in Roscommon and was smitten with your grandmother but could not afford to ask for her hand in marriage. He left Ireland and went to England to find work. He worked as a courier and saved enough money to start his own courier business. Five years later he returned to Ireland to ask your grandmother to marry him and found out she had moved to America and married your grandfather. He moved on and married my grandmother, but once in a while, when he had too many drinks, he would speak of Margaret Donnelly as the love that got away."

Erin was speechless, but after a moment she said, "I didn't know that. My grandmother never mentioned anything about it."

Quinn flashed Erin a charming smile that made her heart flutter and said, "It is a small world, but I am happy to be teaching someone with roots from the same place as my family." Quinn was one of those men who had a naturally smooth, appealing voice. The Irish accent only made his voice that much sexier. Erin imagined that she could listen to him talk for hours. Yet she was confused at why she felt so drawn to him.

Erin quickly reminded herself she had a wonderful husband and that she should not be admiring this handsome Irish bachelor. She tried to refocus and said, "Thank you for taking the time to teach me. What are you going to be talking about tonight?"

Quinn smiled and said, "Yes, my Irish American flower, the topic of the night is a little history lesson in dream travel." Erin settled back in the couch and focused her mind on what she was about to hear. Quinn continued, "Dream travelers have been around since the beginning of time and have learned from their mistakes. The collective knowledge of years of mistakes is what triggered the formation of the DTC. Thus, the DTC is the culmination of thousands of years of experience."

Erin nodded as she imagined the many possible mistakes and errors that could have happened from lifetimes of unstructured dream travel. Quinn went on to review some of the items that Sienna had taught her and added his thoughts regarding Terrents, dream travelers, and Garans.

Quinn uncrossed his legs and stretched them. He took a deep breath and said, "The time continuum is a liquid environment. I think the best way to think of time is as an endless beach of sand. Each particle of sand is a moment of time. Some clumps of sand may stick together—as some of the more significant moments do to form events in time. Everything else in the world—people, all living and nonliving things, weather, and physical laws of the earth—have the ability to affect the placement of the particles of sand...just as they do the moment in time they are exposed to. And in a way similar to particles of sand, some moments in time are on the surface, and if they are moved, they do not disturb the other moments that much. However, there are moments of time similar to a deeply buried particle of sand. These moments are closely linked to many other moments in time, and changing them can affect thousands of other moments of time—similar to how moving a deeply buried particle of sand would cause many other particles above to shift."

Erin absorbed this analogy and asked, "Was Agnes's husband's death one of these deeply buried moments?"

A look of regret crossed Quinn's face, and he softly said, "Yes, I wish there was something we could have done for her. I know it doesn't seem fair to have the gift of dream travel and not to be able to use it when you need it the most." Erin nodded in agreement. Despite the cinnamon they had consumed, their mood became somber.

Erin asked, "How do you determine which moments are the deeply buried ones?"

"We travel back to the moment in question and observe all the elements of the situation. We then have to map each element forward to see the immediate and long-term outcome. As you can imagine, this is an exhausting undertaking requiring one or more of the Garans to travel to the future." Erin sat back farther into the couch and put her feet up on an ottoman in front of her.

Quinn stated, "Another limitation to changing events is that we will only change freshly experienced moments in time. As time passes, the specific moment becomes tied to subsequent moments, and the impact of changing the event would be too substantial."

Erin nodded in understanding and let go of the hope of saving her uncle Sean from dying of colon cancer. She had recently been wondering if she would be allowed to go back and convince him to have a colonoscopy a few years before his diagnosis. Erin knew that the test could have caught the colon cancer before it spread to the other parts of his body.

Erin noticed that, just like Sienna, Quinn spoke of traveling to the future as if it were a disliked chore. Before Erin could question his attitude, Quinn sighed and said in his melodic voice, "Well, my Irish American flower, I should let you get some rest tonight."

Erin nodded and said, "I guess that would be best."

As Quinn leaned forward, a gold triquetra necklace revealed itself.

Erins eyes opened wide in interest as she said, "That is a lovely triquentra! My father wears a triquetra that has been passed down in our family for hundreds of years."

Quinn raised his eyebrows in surprise and replied, "The triquetra is the traditional Celtic symbol of a Garan. Do you see how the three corners create a triangle?"

Erin nodded and said, "Yes, I never noticed that before. My father said that family stories were associated with his triquetra that we were decendents of Celtic druids."

Quinn replied, "I think I have to dig deeper into your family history because it is likely that you had a Garan in your family who has passed down that heirloom."

Erin smiled and said, "That would make sense why there were also family rumors that my father's great-grandmother was considered bizarre for knowing too much."

Quinn smiled playfully and said, "There is so much left to learn about you, but I must send you back. I will see you again next Friday. Lie back and close your eyes."

Erin knew this routine. She said her thank you, lay back on the couch, and closed her eyes. In what felt like just a second, she opened her eyes again in her own bed. Erin looked at the alarm clock and saw that it was 4:10 a.m. She reached out and found Dante's hand and fell back asleep, her mind buzzing with all the information she had just learned.

22

Erin woke up Saturday morning to the sound of Dante taking a shower. She groggily recalled that this was Dante's weekend on call at the hospital. He and the two partners in his practice alternated on-call weekends. Erin pulled herself out of bed a few minutes later as Dante was getting dressed and gave him a hug.

"Good morning," she said.

Dante returned her good-morning hug and greeting and said, "So, are you ready for the big unveiling?"

Erin remembered that they had decided to tell Sandra and their families about Erin's pregnancy today. Erin gulped as she thought about how Sandra might respond to the news. She knew that her family and Dante's family would be excited, but Erin was not sure how Sandra was going to take it.

Erin replied, "Yes, we'll start with Sandra when you get home from work, right?"

Dante replied, "Yes, I was thinking that we could go out to eat at Nicola's Restaurant and give her the news over dinner."

Erin considered the idea and said, "That's probably a good idea because she'll be less likely to freak out in public."

Dante smiled and said, "Exactly. That's what I was thinking. Then when we get home, we can start making the phone calls to our families."

"Sounds good," Erin replied.

Erin walked Dante to the front door and hugged and kissed him good-bye. As she closed the door and went upstairs, she decided that she would distract herself by cleaning their closet. She proceeded to take everything out of the walk-in closet and place it on their bed. Once the closet was empty, she dusted all the shelves and started putting things back in the closet in an organized fashion.

When Sandra got home from her sleepover, Erin told her that they were going to dinner at half past six. Sandra looked exhausted and briefly agreed before going to her room to take a nap. Erin had taken a few breaks from her project to eat breakfast and lunch, but she realized at half past four that she still hadn't showered. The closet had been a bigger task than she had estimated, but it had kept Erin away from Sandra most of the day, which was good since she was so nervous about the unveiling at dinner. Erin quickly finished putting the last few items back in the closet and jumped into the shower. She was almost finished blow-drying her hair when Dante walked in and gave her a hug and kiss.

Minutes later, they drove two minutes to Nicola's and were settled into a small table in the back corner of the restaurant. Nicola's restaurant was small, but about sixteen tables fit comfortably in the dining area. The restaurant was decorated tastefully with the rustic colors of old-world Italy. The decor and dim lighting created a cozy, intimate setting for dinner.

After placing their orders, Erin and Dante looked at each other, and Dante began the talk that Erin had been dreading all day. "Sandra, we have some news that we want to share with you."

Sandra looked at Erin and Dante and said, "You're pregnant, right?"

Erin was a little surprised by the accuracy of the question and said, "Yes, how did you know?"

Sandra nonchalantly responded, "I just guessed. I haven't seen you drink wine with dinner for the past few weeks, and you seem to be going to bed early lately. Nicole's mom did the same thing two years ago when she was pregnant." Sandra paused and said, "And you don't have to worry about me being upset. I can't say I'm happy about not being the only child anymore, but it will be fun to have a cute baby around to hold."

Erin exhaled and felt like a ton of bricks just lifted from her shoulders. When the waiter finished pouring their sparkling water, they held up their glasses and said, "Cheers!" Erin and Dante were not a typical family, but Erin felt that, no matter what, Sandra and Dante were hers, and she loved them for who they were.

When they arrived home after dinner, Erin and Dante began the task of making phone calls to family members to tell them the news. Everyone was happy when they heard and wished Erin and Dante well. It came as no surprise to Erin when their excited relatives asked if they were going to find out the gender of the baby ahead of time and if they had thought of any names yet.

Although Erin and Dante hadn't actually started discussing names, they both agreed that they would wait and be surprised with the baby's gender at the birth. Erin guessed that both Dante and his parents were secretly hoping for a boy, but Erin didn't care what the gender was. She was just looking forward to meeting her little baby. Erin went to bed that night thinking about baby names.

Sandra's mother picked her up on Sunday morning for an overnight stay. With Dante working at the hospital, Erin had the whole day to herself. She spent Sunday morning doing laundry and organizing the file cabinet where she stored her bills and paperwork. She had a few weeks' worth of paid bills stacked on top of the file cabinet that needed to be filed, and she always felt better when everything was organized and put in its place. As Erin sorted through the papers, she saw a security-assurance message saying that her credit card company had the most secure database in the industry.

Erin remembered that she had heard Rayna say that there was a new version of the Terrent database that the DTs were able to use, and she realized that she didn't know how to access that database yet. Erin quickly finished up the filing and booted the desktop computer.

Erin opened her personal e-mail and typed a message to Sienna asking how things were going with the new dream traveler and when she would have access to the Terrent database. Erin included an update that stated that things were going well with Quinn and that she missed getting to chat with Sienna. Erin hit Send and shut down the computer. She spent the rest of the day cleaning and cooking Dante's favorite dinner of steak, sautéed spinach, and sweet potatoes. Dante came home at five o'clock, and they were able to spend a nice, romantic evening alone. Erin fell asleep Sunday night feeling content and happy.

23

Monday morning started as most Mondays did, with Erin sighing when she woke up and realized that it was only the first day of the workweek. She showered and then walked into the closet and picked out her black slacks and burgundy sweater to wear. She experienced a practical, little reminder of her pregnancy when she couldn't button the top button of slacks, which were her favorite pair. Erin switched to a pair of gray slacks that were a larger size, but she recognized that she would soon need to buy maternity clothes for work. She had decided that she would be telling her manager, Ronan, that she was pregnant today, and she went through her morning routine slightly distracted and a little nervous.

Erin worried during her commute to work that her revelation would ruin her chance of getting the promotion she was due; however, she was starting to show, and she wanted to be the one to tell Ronan instead of him hearing it through rumor. Erin arrived at work and walked into the building, thinking that at least she wouldn't have to hide her pregnancy anymore, and it would be a relief to talk freely about the baby.

By the time she had reached her desk, her mood had changed, and she was feeling better. She e-mailed Ronan to see if he could meet for a few minutes, and Ronan accepted her invite via his BlackBerry and messaged back that he was on his way into the office, and she could be his first appointment. A few minutes later, just as Erin was about to walk to Ronan's office, Molly came in, smiling from ear to ear.

Erin said, "Good morning, you look happy!"

"I am happy! I have good news!" Molly responded.

Molly's happiness was contagious, and Erin couldn't help smiling as she said, "I have good news, too."

Molly was almost jumping with joy, but she insisted that Erin share her news first. "Well, I am on my way to officially tell Ronan, but I would rather tell you first. I'm pregnant."

Molly let out a scream of glee and hugged Erin as she said, "That *is* great news! Congratulations! I am so happy for you! My good news is rather like yours: my sister is pregnant, too, and I am going to be an aunt! I can't wait. Now I have two babies to look forward to! That's why Ronan took my family away for the weekend—so that he and my sister, Kerry, could share the good news. It will be my parents' first grandchild, so they couldn't be happier. My sister is due July twenty-eighth. When are you due?"

Erin responded, "My due date is July seventeenth! Wow! We are due at almost the same time!"

Molly was so happy she was bouncing on her heels. "I am so excited!" she said. "I can't wait to see these babies. You will still be here in May and June for study-database lock and to hear the results, right?"

Erin answered, "Yes, if everything goes according to plan, I will try to work up until the very end of my pregnancy." As Erin mentioned the end of the study, she made the connection to Ronan's change of leadership style and said, "Molly, Ronan's dramatic change makes sense now."

Molly nodded slightly and answered, "Ronan seems so much happier in general now. I guess he really wanted to be a father. My sister doesn't seem to be affected as much—if anything she seemed a little surprised by the pregnancy—but Ronan is just all smiles." Molly looked at her watch and said, "Oh, I have to run to a meeting, but we'll catch up more later. Congratulations, again!" And she turned and walked briskly down the hallway.

Erin took a deep breath and gathered her notepad, a pen, and her BlackBerry. Just as she took a few steps toward the hallway, Erin heard a ringing in her ears that made her pause. She thought how different her life was now that she knew that the ringing represented a dream traveler in the near vicinity. The ringing sound subsided, but Erin kept wondering which dream traveler was in the area. As Erin was walking, she saw Sarah running down the end of the hallway before turning down the left branch. Erin felt guilty about not talking to Sarah for weeks, and she made a mental note to stop by and visit her soon.

Erin continued on to Ronan's office and saw that his office light was off and his office was empty. She returned to her desk, sat down, and began to go through her e-mails. About ten minutes later, she heard heavy footsteps as Ronan quickly approached her desk, slightly short of breath, and said, "I'm sorry, Erin. I was stuck in traffic. I have about ten minutes before my next meeting; do you still want to meet now?" Ronan's face was red and shiny with perspiration.

Erin quickly replied, "Yes, that will be perfect. I just need a minute of your time." She gathered up her stuff again and followed Ronan to his office.

Erin started to feel nervous again as she watched Ronan take off his coat and settle into his chair. She closed the door to the office behind her, sat in one of chairs in front of his desk, and nervously folded her hands on her lap. She then quickly said, "I just wanted to inform you that I am pregnant. I plan on working during my whole pregnancy and on returning to work after my maternity leave, and I hope that I will not burden the team too much with my absence."

Ronan almost looked more relaxed after Erin shared the news than he had before. He smiled and said, "That is wonderful news! Congratulations! I'm not sure if you have talked to Molly yet, but my wife is also pregnant."

Erin felt a wave of relief and responded, "Molly just told me a little while ago. She was practically jumping for joy when she came in this morning. She said your wife is due July twenty-eighth, and I'm actually due July seventeenth."

Ronan leaned forward in his chair and looked at Erin with a concerned expression and said, "I just want you to know that everyone here will be available to support you. Things here can get stressful sometimes, so please feel free to take breaks if you need them, and step out for doctor's appointments or anything else you need. Please let me know if there is anything else that I can do to make sure you're comfortable during the next few months."

Erin could not have been happier with his response and was close to tearing up when she said, "Thank you so much. I really appreciate it." Erin looked at her watch and realized it was time for Ronan's next meeting. She stood up and said, "I don't want to keep you from your next meeting. Thanks again for all your support." Erin closed Ronan's door behind her and walked back to her desk, feeling completely relieved that she didn't have to hide her pregnancy anymore and that her boss had responded so well to the news.

Erin's day continued to go smoothly, and she was able to catch up on reviewing reports during the morning. In the afternoon Erin had a teleconference with the regional study managers and discussed the recent drop in study enrollment. Everyone had hoped that the enrollment would pick up after the holidays; however, it had remained low, and the goal of finishing the study in May was now at risk. Erin desperately wanted to complete the study enrollment in May so that she could complete the database lock before she left for maternity leave, and she began reviewing ideas for how to help the sites screen more patients.

Erin knew that the staff members who worked at their study sites were very busy, and they worked on multiple clinical trials. However, the slow enrollment was frustrating because if Erin's study drug worked and saved people who were dying from pancreatic cancer—as early indications showed was likely—then every day that the study was delayed would mean delays in when the study drug would be available to patients who needed it. The clinical-research field was heavily regulated, and these regulations required the site staff to complete and maintain tremendous amounts of paperwork. Unfortunately, due to the medical-compliance laws in place, Erin's company was very restricted in how they could help study sites screen and enroll patients in their studies.

Erin was also aware that in the 1990s pharmaceutical sales and marketing representatives provided excessive, lavish gifts to doctors in efforts to boost their district sales numbers. Unfortunately, several of these poor examples impacted the public's opinion of all pharmaceutical employees. Erin felt that this impression was unfair. Many other people were at pharmaceutical companies, like Erin, who worked hard to find new medications and cures. Erin desperately wanted to help free up the study-site staff's time so that they could look for patients for her study, but giving the study site equipment or money to hire someone to help them complete paperwork was considered a gift and was not allowed by law.

Erin and all the regional-study managers on the teleconference call resolved to brainstorm ideas to help the sites screen more patients and boost enrollment. They agreed to regroup in a week and share their ideas. Erin answered e-mails for the rest of the afternoon and went through her normal evening routine of picking up Sandra from school and buying and making dinner. When Erin lay down in bed, she realized that, even though it was only Monday, she was already exhausted.

Erin met with Dr. Ruben on Tuesday afternoon for a brief checkup visit. He said he was happy with how things were progressing and that her weight gain of two pounds was normal and on target. Erin knew that it was normal and healthy to gain weight during pregnancy, but she did not like watching the scale creep up. She was already planning a strategy for how to lose weight after the baby was born.

The rest of the week was uneventful, and by Friday afternoon Erin was looking forward to meeting with Quinn. Over the past week, she had found herself frequently wondering about the things he had told her, especially the fact that his grandfather had been in love with her grandmother. All of Erin's grandparents, except for her paternal grandmother, Nanny, had passed away before Erin was five years old, so she had been especially drawn to Nanny. And Nanny had been the ideal grandmother who baked her Irish soda bread each time Erin visited and spoiled her with ice cream and with butterscotch candy. Erin had wonderful memories of Nanny, and she felt the loss of her grandmother dramatically when she had passed away ten years ago.

Erin was also thinking about how Quinn had explained that moments in time were like particles of sand. Erin was still having trouble understanding all the variables involved with events in time and how the DTC determined which ones should or should not be altered. She had gone from being a regular participant in the world to someone with the ability to both participate and observe simultaneously, and she was not quite used to the feeling.

As Erin got ready for bed on Friday night, she thought about Quinn's teaching style. He had been very knowledgeable and open with her, and she determined to use her time with him to learn as much as possible about this new world of dream travel. Of course, Erin also made sure that she focused only on the outfit she wanted to travel in when she fell asleep.

24

She was dreaming about walking on the beach by the ocean. It was foggy, and she was staring at the rough waves hitting the shoreline when she slipped into a sand hole, and her arms flew up reflexively in the air. It was too late to catch herself, and she landed softly in the moist peat moss a second later. When Erin opened her eyes, she recognized the stone wall to her left from the last time she had traveled to Quinn's home. Looking down at herself she saw, with a sigh of relief, that she was wearing the brown sweater, blue jeans, brown leather boots, and wool jacket she had planned to wear. Erin stood up and looked at the ocean. It was a much clearer day than the last time she had traveled there. When she glanced back a second later, she saw Quinn standing by the entrance of the wall with a large grin on his face and a green wool blanket folded in his arms.

Erin walked closer, smiling as she pointed at herself and said, "I did a little better planning for this trip."

Quinn pointed at the wool blanket in his hands and said, "I came prepared this time." He added, "You look nice, but I can't help saying that I was hoping you would be planning another tropical vacation as you fell asleep."

Quinn's flirting maintained such a genuine innocence that Erin felt flattered and yet comfortable. He pointed toward the door to his home and said, "Should I carry you for old time's sake?"

Erin giggled and answered, "Thank you, but I think I can manage."

They walked together through the open metal entrance gate and up to the front door. Erin had not seen the walkway the last time, but she noted that Quinn had an actual moat surrounding his home. The entrance walkway was a metal-framed, flat structure, about ten feet wide, with large wood planks lined together to form the walking surface. The place where the walkway met the front of Quinn's home looked like it was on some type of retractable track that pulled back into the structure.

Quinn noticed her line of vision and asked, "Do you like my Garan security system?"

Erin smiled and said, "Let me guess: I bet that moat is filled with fluoridated water, right?"

Quinn chuckled and answered, "Of course!"

Quinn stepped in front of Erin and opened the large, beautifully ornate, dark wood front door. He stood to the side and bowed slightly as he stretched out his left hand in a welcoming gesture and said, "After you, my dear."

Erin smiled and stepped across the threshold. She looked around slowly and admired the front hallway she had missed the last time she came. The hallway was about three stories high and had a beautiful, old-fashioned candle and crystal chandelier. Large tapestries with village scenes from the Middle Ages were hanging on the sidewalls. The wall that faced the front door featured a large painting of a robust woman with chocolate-brown hair, a pale but rosy-cheeked complexion, and sky-blue eyes. By the design of the dress and the woman's hairstyle, Erin guessed the painting was from the 1920s.

Erin saw the entrance to the living room that she had been in last time to her left, and she began walking in that direction. With the heavy drapes blocking the little daylight available, the room was darker than the front hallway, but the fire in the fireplace was crackling cozily, and several candles casted a soft red glow about the room. Erin walked toward the couch she had sat on last time and smelled the fragrance of cinnamon-scented candles. She had the impulse to tease Quinn about the cinnamon, but she decided to transition to a professional mood. Quinn gestured to the couch, and when Erin was seated, Quinn sat on a chair across from her.

Quinn leaned back, stretched his legs out in front of him, and said, "I think we had a productive session last week. I know it was a lot of information to digest. Do you have any questions about anything we covered?"

"Actually, I noticed that both you and Sienna have referred to future travel in a negative fashion," Erin replied. "I would think it would be so interesting to see what it's like in the future. For instance, I'm working really hard on a study right now, and I don't know if all my hard work will result in getting a new medication for pancreatic cancer approved by the FDA. I would love to go into the future and see if my study drug works. But it seems like you and Sienna are uncomfortable with it. Do you dislike traveling to the future?"

Quinn's expression grew more serious, and he answered, "Seeing the future is dangerous because it impacts how we think and behave in current time. Thus, we Garans try to do the least amount of future travel as possible."

Erin nodded in agreement, but Quinn's expression grew more intense as he said, "Imagine what a burden it would be to have future knowledge of a friend's or loved one's impending tragedy—like a death from a sudden heart attack—and not to be able to warn the person to get their things in order or to say their good-byes.

"In addition we can't talk about it or share our knowledge with anyone because it would be wrong to force another to share the burden of that knowledge with us. It's a curse to have knowledge of a future event and not to be able to talk about it or do anything to prevent it. Then, when the event takes place, it's easy to feel as if we almost caused the tragedy."

From the intense way Quinn described future travel, she wondered if he had to endure such a burden. Erin fully grasped the severity from Quinn's description and said, "I never thought of it that way. I only thought it would be nice to peek into the future and see what things were like. I never realized the implications of having that knowledge." Erin paused for a minute and asked, "What about when Terrents hijack a dream traveler and see a time in the future from their own local time?"

Quinn nodded and said, "Ah yes, Terrent hijackers do travel forward to a time in the future from their local time, but hijacker time travel isn't precise. Due to the nature of their travel, they can steer toward a year they would like to visit, but the place and exact date are random, and because of the chaotic situation caused by dream traveler's resistance, they can wind up anywhere on the planet in that given year.

"Also, they are usually only there for a few seconds or minutes before dream travelers are able to wake up on their own. Thus, Terrents usually only get to observe glimpses of the future. They take whatever information they can gather back to their Terrent organization, the Tara League. The Tara League accumulates the knowledge in order to develop anything that can profit the Terrents. Terrents have profited from their advances in technology—based on glimpses of the future—so much that they are some of the most powerful and wealthy individuals in the world."

"How does the DTC use the information collected from the Terrent-identification visits, like the one I did weeks ago?"

Quinn replied, "Good question. Finding Terrents is a difficult practice. Once we know the identity of a Terrent, we start researching the branches of his or her family for other Terrents. We research a place to visit suspected Terrents when they were young children and away from the parents, and their reaction to our presence confirms or disproves our suspicion. Once they are in our database, we track all available information to document where Terrents live and work each year. The knowledge we are gathering currently will be used in the future to help DTs travel back in time safely."

Erin was still astonished by this parallel universe of dream travelers and Terrents that she was learning more about. A few months ago, she had been completely ignorant of this alternate world, and now she was learning while she herself dream traveled to an island off the coast of Ireland! Erin sighed at her thoughts, and Quinn took this as a signal to continue.

"We have also had success performing identification visits to all known inventors and leaders in technology. At least fifty percent of inventors are Terrents. The third most successful method we have is using information gathered from dental insurance databases. We track people who have a higher-than-average number of cavities. The absence of any fluoride can make a predictable, negative effect on dental health, and these people usually need a lot of dental work or may even lose their teeth earlier in life."

Erin was thinking about the possibilities while Quinn was talking, and when he paused for breath, she blurted out, "Do Terrents have discomfort around someone dream traveling from the time they are born?"

Quinn was surprised at her interruption but immediately answered, "Yes. As far as we know, Terrents have the same reaction from the time they are born until the time they die."

Erin's expression brightened, and she said, "Part of my student rotation when I was studying to become a nurse included spending a few months working in a hospital maternity ward. All the nursing students in my class had to spend several days in the newborn nursery to learn about the role of the nursery nurse. Many babies born in a hospital in the United States spend several hours away from the parents in a nursery, having vital signs taken and being weighed. A nursery with twenty to thirty newborns would be a wonderful place to test for Terrents, while the children are too young to remember but are away from their parents."

Quinn looked like a proud father as he realized the potential for Erin's nursery-identification-visit idea. He replied in his sexy Irish accent, "Erin, I think you have just hit upon a wonderful idea!"

Erin stood up to emphasize her point and said, "The housekeeping staff is the least noticeable in most settings. If a dream traveler were to wear a housekeeping uniform, he or she should be able to walk through the nursery without bothering anyone except for the babies who are Terrents. If the dream traveler keeps track of all the babies who react by crying and squirming, we should be able to follow up on many more Terrents."

Quinn stood up also and began pacing back and forth, digesting all the possible benefits of the idea. "Would you mind if I brought this idea back to the DTC? I will, of course, let everyone know that it's your idea, but I think it's a great idea that needs to be shared."

Erin's cheeks blushed, and she happily responded, "Yes, that's fine. It's just an idea, but I hope it helps the greater cause."

"I think your wonderful idea will help us all!" Quinn replied. His excitement must have gotten the best of him because he stopped in front of Erin, and in one swift movement, he put his hands on her shoulders and pulled her close. Erin's body instantly betrayed her, and she felt herself grow warmer in response to Quinn's possessive gesture. Her face and her body language definitely sent the wrong signal because Quinn took her face in his hands and gently touched his lips to hers. Erin had a moment of pleasure that was followed by a tidal wave of guilt.

"This is wrong!" Erin said as soon as she pulled away from the kiss. She felt like a traitor and couldn't make eye contact with Quinn.

"I am an idiot; that was entirely my fault. I acted from too much cinnamon followed by too much excitement. Please forgive me!"

Erin sat down heavily on the couch and rubbed her forehead. She could not believe that she had just let herself enjoy a kiss with someone other than her husband. Her only defense was to accept the cinnamon excuse and to start convincing herself that it was totally the effects of the cinnamon that had allowed her response, not a lapse in her loyalty to her husband.

Quinn sat back down and said, "OK, we now know that mixing excitement and cinnamon is a dangerous idea; we should not let that happen again! Let me send you back so that you can get some rest. I think it is fair to say that we have done enough work tonight. I will see you again next Friday, Erin. Go ahead and lie back and close your eyes."

Erin put her feet on the ottoman, rested against the cushions of the sofa, and closed her eyes. In one swift moment, she was back in her bed, lying next to her husband. Erin was still upset and felt unsettled that Quinn had winked at her when he had said, "We should not let that happen again!"

25

E rin opened her eyes and tried to adjust to the moonlight that streamed around the window shades. Their bedroom was still dark, but she saw the outline of Dante's innocent face, and she instantly felt a fresh wave of guilt. Erin tried to fall back to sleep, but she couldn't. Although it was the harder choice, she decided to tell Dante the truth about what she had just done. Erin knew that lies will destroy a relationship and that the right thing to do was to be honest and let Dante know she had made a mistake.

Erin gently rubbed Dante's arm and whispered, "Dante. Babe, can you wake up for a second?"

Dante coughed, rubbed his eyes, and rolled to face Erin in bed. "What's wrong?"

Erin was afraid of Dante's possible reaction, but she said, "I just returned from dream traveling to an island off Ireland, from the house of a Garan named Quinn." Erin paused when she saw the confused look on Dante's face, but she forged ahead. "Well, there were cinnamon candles burning, and then we were talking about an exciting dream-travel idea, and then we kissed. I'm sorry, Dante. I feel horrible about it. Maybe it was because of the cinnamon, but I guess that's not an adequate excuse." Erin waited for Dante's reaction.

Dante raised his eyebrows and said, "That's it? You woke me because you kissed someone in your sleep? Seriously, Erin, do you know how many times I have dreamed about being with other women? That's why it's called dreaming. However, I would rather not hear about your dreams about other men, so in the future, please don't wake me from a sound sleep to tell me about them. And I don't want to hear you talk about this dream-traveling thing anymore." Dante rolled over to face the opposite direction and firmly said, "Good night."

Erin responded, "Good night." Then she relaxed back in bed.

Erin felt relieved that she had told Dante, but she knew that dream traveling did not fall into the same category as regular dreaming, which was controlled by the subconscious. Erin was in control of her behavior during dream travel. She could use the excuse that, after all, it was Quinn who had kissed her, but she had definitely been an active participant by letting the kiss continue longer than she should have.

Erin was still confused by her attraction to Quinn, but she felt a lot better since Dante had basically given her permission to do whatever she wanted while she slept. Part of Erin knew that this perception was not right, but she closed her eyes and fell back to sleep, thinking that she would see Quinn again in one week. She was apprehensive, yet excited.

Erin spent the weekend in a state of confusion. She knew that she loved Dante, and she did not want to hurt him, but she kept thinking about Quinn, despite her best efforts not to. Erin wondered if it had something to do with the parallel world of dream travel. Before she was aware of her dream-traveler gift, she was completely satisfied with her husband. Was it her existence in two worlds that fueled her attraction to a man who shared her dream-traveler world? Was it something to do with her pregnancy hormones?

Erin was grateful that Dante did not bring up the subject all weekend, but she couldn't help feeling extremely guilty when she looked at him. The weekend dragged by with Erin in a fog of guilt, and by Sunday night she was almost looking forward to going back to work to get her mind off the whole thing.

Unfortunately, Erin soon found out that work did not distract her enough, and she spent each day of the workweek counting off the days until Quinn would be summoning her.

When Friday evening finally arrived, Erin was so excited that she had trouble falling asleep. She spent hours thinking about the right outfit to wear and finally settled on black jeans, black boots, and a blue scoop-neck sweater. She didn't want to look like she was trying to impress Quinn, and this outfit would look nice without appearing she put too much effort into it.

Erin vowed to stay focused on what she had to learn and to make sure that Quinn understood that the kiss was a mistake that Erin did not plan on repeating. After a long time, Erin finally fell asleep.

26

Erin dreamed that she was trying to climb a mountain, but the surface was muddy and slippery and she kept slowly sliding backward. Time after time she ended up where she had started, until one rapid slide backward dropped Erin onto a soft, moist surface.

Erin opened her eyes and saw that she was outside Quinn's stone wall. She stood up, dusted herself off, and happily noticed she was wearing the right outfit. She was a little surprised that she could notice her tiny pregnancy bump when she looked down.

There was a thick fog, but when Erin walked to the entrance gate, she saw Quinn standing in his doorway, waiting. As Erin crossed the bridge, she saw that Quinn had a questioning look in his eyes and was hesitantly smiling at her. Erin knew that any type of greeting would be awkward, and she avoided the need to greet him with a hug or to shake his hand by pointing to the tapestries just as she was about to cross the threshold. "I meant to say last week that those are beautiful tapestries! Are they family heirlooms?"

Quinn looked relieved by the distraction. He closed the door, followed her into the front hallway, and answered, "Oh…no, I guess you can say they are Garan heirlooms that I inherited. They are beautiful, but they are a bit of a nuisance to properly maintain."

Erin acknowledged his response with a nod, and they both walked into the living room and sat in their normal seats. Erin noticed with relief that there was a fire in the fireplace but no candles burning.

The awkward feeling continued for a moment before Quinn broke the silence and said, "OK, let us begin. The main topic I want to cover tonight is the unusual circumstances around dream travel. For instance, the inability to dream travel and interact with a pregnant woman."

Erin's expression reflected her surprise, and she said, "I didn't realize that. So if I wanted to go back to visit the version of myself from a week ago, I couldn't?"

Quinn replied, "You can observe, but the version of yourself in that current physical time will not be able to see your dream-traveler self or any other dream travelers because a pregnant woman cannot hear or see anyone who is dream traveling.

"We are not sure why this happens, but it's a universal fact for all pregnant women. It is strange because pregnant DTs can dream travel, be summoned by Garans, and, unfortunately, be hijacked by Terrents. However, a pregnant dream traveler in her own current time cannot hear or see a person in a dream-traveler state."

Erin processed this new information and wondered what kept pregnant woman from being able to see dream travelers.

Quinn crossed his legs and said, "Sienna told you that she sensed your first DT experience. I want to explain that a little further. All Garans have an extra sense that is tied into the time continuum. Garans have the ability to sense when a dream traveler causes a change in history. It is usually how we find new dream travelers. Once a Garan feels this hiccup in the time continuum caused by a dream traveler, we focus on the source of the sensation. The Garans can typically follow the sensation, or dream-traveler energy, as it exits the dream travel to the time and place of the sleeping dream traveler.

"By the time you woke up from your interaction with your dad in 1968, we were able to estimate your geographical location—all from your energy sensation. The DTC then used that information to search numerous computer databases to determine your name and to perform more research on you and your family."

Erin nodded in understanding as she digested this information. The DTC had found her so quickly after her first DT experience that she had figured something similar to this must have occurred.

Quinn continued, "Another unusual circumstance is one that you know all too well—the delayed discovery of one's dream-traveler gift. Occasionally, the hormone spike of puberty does not trigger the DT gift, and it's triggered later in life by a pregnancy or thyroid disturbance. My friend Ted—the fellow who appeared in just his boxer shorts at the DTC party—actually became a dream traveler at the age of forty-five, after experiencing a chemical imbalance from a benign growth on his thyroid."

Erin smiled thinking about Ted. Quinn considering Ted not just a dream traveler but also his friend was a nice example of Quinn's nonjudgmental character.

Quinn continued, "I am not sure if Sienna already covered this, but you should know that a DT version of yourself can only visit a particular time and place one time. Once you visit, your DT self becomes part of that time period and place. There cannot be two DT versions of yourself in the same time and place.

"For example, Sienna told me that you performed the Terrent-identification visit for Jerry Lamar. You will never be able to dream travel to that exact time and place again. That is why we try to be as strategic as possible when we plan our Terrent-identification visits. We only have a limited number of DTs working, and we want to utilize their DT visits as efficiently as possible."

Erin was a little overwhelmed by this concept, but she decided to think about the whole idea further before asking any questions. She sadly realized that she would never again be able to visit the night of her first kiss with Dante. As Erin thought about that dream-travel experience, she felt the now-familiar guilt as she looked into Quinn's eyes and remembered their kiss.

Quinn must have sensed the change in Erin's mood. He looked slightly apologetic as he took a deep breath, leaned back an inch, and said, "Lastly, I just want to say, again, that I am sorry for my behavior last week." Quinn's eyes lost their playful twinkle and the corners of his mouth drew down into a pained expression as he continued. "Obviously, I'm attracted to you; however, I'm aware that you're not only married but pregnant. My behavior last week was selfish and wrong. I think it's best that I limit my exposure to you moving forward. Sienna will finish the intense dream-traveler training for the new DT, Layla, in the next day or two, and then she will take over your weekly sessions after tonight."

Erin could tell that Quinn was being honest, and she felt flattered that he was attracted to her. She was torn between disappointment and relief over the fact that she would not be coming back, and she could only respond, "Oh. OK."

Erin knew this session was over. Although she didn't want to say good-bye this way, she knew it was for the best. She pushed back into the sofa she usually sat on, put her feet up on the ottoman, and closed her eyes.

"I really do appreciate everything you have done," Erin quickly said. "Thank you, Quinn."

With her eyes still closed, she heard a soft whisper from Quinn in his sexy Irish brogue. "Good-bye, my Irish American flower."

Erin quickly opened her eyes, not sure how she should respond, but she immediately saw that she was back in her own room, in bed next to Dante. With a sigh of mixed relief and regret, Erin realized that she would not see Quinn in an intimate setting again. Their experience together had been brief and, thankfully, mostly innocent. Erin didn't know exactly how to feel, so she decided to just remember how special Quinn made her feel. The reminder that she was of Irish descent and the fact that Quinn highly desired her made her feel better about herself. She fell asleep thinking of what her life might have been like if she had been born in Ireland, instead of in the United States.

27

Erin spent the rest of her weekend trying not to think about Quinn, and once again, she was grateful to be going to work when she woke up on Monday morning.

Once she was arrived at work and was settled in her office, Erin booted up her computer and scanned the list of e-mails in her inbox. She noticed an e-mail from Ronan with the subject line "Dinner with Friends." Erin clicked on the e-mail and saw an invitation for her and Dante to join Ronan and his wife for dinner at Ronan's house on Wednesday night. Erin thought about her plans for the week and realized that she and Dante were free that night, but she wasn't sure how she felt about dinner at Ronan's house. However, Erin really appreciated how wonderful Ronan had been when she notified him of her pregnancy, and she knew that she could not turn down his invitation.

On Wednesday night at six o'clock, Dante pulled the car into the circular driveway of the address Ronan had given them in Franklin Lakes, New Jersey. Dante whistled and said, "Nice house!" The historic, southern-style home had a red brick exterior and was almost twice as large as their house.

Erin and Dante slowly walked up to the front door, taking in the beautifully designed double oak doors. Seconds after Dante pressed the doorbell, Ronan greeted them and ushered them into his home, shaking Dante's hand as he stepped over the threshold. As Ronan took their coats, Erin noticed the expensive-looking artwork displayed in the front hall.

Erin had been able to find a black baby-doll dress that still fit her. It somewhat camouflaged her baby bump with a plunging neckline that accentuated her chest. Erin tried to feel confident in her own beauty as she followed Ronan through the front hall and into the kitchen, but she realized she was fighting a losing battle when she spotted Ronan's beautiful wife, Kerry, who stood up as they approached.

Erin was surprised at how different Ronan's wife looked from Molly. She had a pale complexion similar to Molly's, but she had wavy, shoulder-length raven hair and deep-brown eyes. She was wearing a red satin slip dress with geisha-type designs on the neckline. Erin saw that she had a perfect petite body with a small baby bump. Erin immediately felt bloated in her presence.

Kerry greeted them by saying, "After hearing about you from Molly, it is so nice to finally meet you in person, Erin. And this must be your husband, Dante." Kerry smiled and shook both of their hands as she said, "It is a pleasure to meet you both!"

The two couples exchanged small talk as Erin quickly admired the expansive kitchen that featured granite countertops laid out in a squared-off *U* shape framing a restaurant-sized steel stove top and oven.

Kerry guided them to the dining room off to the right and said, "Please, come sit down." The walls of the dining room were a deep, warm burgundy, and the color complimented the lavish cherrywood dining room furniture. Kerry signaled for everyone to sit down and said, "I heard that we are both due at almost the same time." Erin sat down in the chair across from Kerry, and they began sharing their pregnancy experiences.

Erin was pleasantly surprised that dinner conversation flowed so easily. Dante and Ronan spoke about the upcoming baseball season and shared their opinions about the New York Yankees and New York Mets players. Erin found Kerry's company very pleasant and thought that she was easy to talk to. They had their due dates in common, and both had chosen to wait and be surprised with their babies' gender at birth.

Erin finally said, "I keep trying to see similarities between you and Molly, and it's an interesting challenge because you are very different from each other."

"I know." Kerry nodded. "I used to tease her that she was adopted because I look like a combination of my parents, and she looks like neither of them."

Even Kerry's mannerisms were completely different from Molly's. Where Molly was impulsive, Kerry was subdued; Kerry was much more polished in how she presented herself.

Erin actually enjoyed the dinner overall, and she was glad that Dante had a chance to meet Ronan in person. They all ended the dinner by agreeing that they must meet again, and Erin actually looked forward to it.

As they drove home, Erin asked, "What did you think of Ronan?"

Dante hesitated for a moment and said, "He was fine."

Erin smiled to herself because she was accustomed to Dante's brief responses to questions like the one she asked. She found how different men were from women humorous. Most women wanted to discuss everything they perceived, and most men just summarized with phrases like Dante's response.

The weeks trickled by, and Erin was not summoned by Sienna. By late February, Erin started to wonder if something was wrong. It had been almost a month since her last training session with Quinn, and Sienna had not tried to reach out to her. Erin sat down in front of her computer one night and debated how she should word an e-mail to Sienna without appearing too needy.

As Erin drafted the e-mail, she felt a quick tickling sensation around her lower abdomen. She stopped typing, lifted her shirt, and rested both of her hands on her baby bump. Less than five seconds later, she felt the same fluttering sensation and realized with joy that she was feeling the baby move.

At her checkup visit the day before, Dr. Ruben had mentioned that she would be feeling the baby move very soon. However, actually feeling her baby's movement was a special milestone for Erin. She smiled and felt an even stronger connection with the baby growing inside her. Erin put her shirt back down, quickly typed a brief message to Sienna, and hit the Send Message button.

Erin became absorbed in her work and her pregnancy planning, and she thought less and less about dream traveling. Erin and Dante had fallen into a regular pattern of meeting up with Ronan and Kerry almost every week to have dinner. Erin was so distracted that she was surprised when she realized a month had passed when she finally received an e-mail reply from Sienna.

Date Sent: March 26, 2004 4:50 p.m.
From: S.Goodman@dmail.com
Subject: Hello

Dear Erin,
I am so sorry for this delay in responding to your e-mail. Please accept my apology for not following up with you sooner. I will not be able to meet with you for a little while longer, but I will explain everything in person the next time I summon you.
—Sienna

Erin sighed as she read the e-mail. Erin had heard other people say that they began to "nest" when they were pregnant, and she was beginning to understand the feeling. She was starting to focus on everything that she wanted to have in place before the birth. She convinced herself that this lack of contact with Sienna was for the best since there was so much going on with her pregnancy and at work.

28

Weeks later, Erin heard Molly packing up her bag to leave work and saw that it was half past five. Erin said, "Wait for me. I will walk out with you." Erin grabbed her purse from her desk drawer and put her laptop in her workbag. She was reminded of her pregnancy when she stood up and felt the still-surprising heaviness of her body. Although there were some negative aspects to being pregnant, like the constant fatigue and indigestion, Erin actually loved being pregnant. She felt that she had some connection to the earth with this miracle blossoming inside her.

"I can't believe we are almost done with the study," Molly said as they walked to the parking lot together.

Erin nodded and said, "I don't want to jinx it, but it's looking like we'll be able to finish ahead of schedule and have the last patient complete the study before the end of this month."

Molly asked, "It's April twentieth today; do you really think we could finish by the thirtieth?"

Erin answered, "I hope so. However, things will get even crazier. The database lock is the end of the trial. It's an exciting time because as soon as we finish cleaning the study data, we'll be able to unlock the study and see which patients received the study drug and which patients received a placebo. Despite the excitement, it can be the most stressful time because everyone has to work feverishly to clean the data."

Molly looked slightly nervous as she processed the idea of an even more intense work environment. She shook her head to dismiss her worry and said, "Kerry told me that she really enjoys spending time with you and Dante."

Erin smiled and said, "She is wonderful. It's great to talk with her because she seems to be experiencing the same pregnancy stuff I am at almost the same time." Erin paused and then said with a teasing smile, "Although I'm mad at her because I look like a fat whale and she looks perfectly thin except for her little baby bump."

Molly started laughing and said, "You look great, but I can sympathize. I have been dieting since I was a teenager, and Kerry has never been on a diet. Yet she manages to somehow look perfect even when she is over six months pregnant!"

Molly looked happy that Erin and her sister were friends and said, "Kerry said that she was working on trying to convince you to deliver at home with a nurse midwife like she is planning to do."

Erin nodded and said, "It does sound nice to be able to have a natural birth at home, but Dr. Ruben would prefer that I be at the hospital in case of an emergency, and Dante agrees with him. Although, I promised Kerry that I would continue to try and convince them both that I should deliver at home, so it may still be an option."

As Erin reached her car, she opened the driver's side door and placed her bags inside before saying, "Have a good night, Molly. I will see you tomorrow."

Molly wished Erin a good night back, and they both got into their cars.

29

For the next five weeks, Erin worked almost every day—including weekends. Study-team members divided spreadsheets of data amoung themselves. Everyone helped review and scrutinize the blinded study data. It was the same process that Erin had done in the past, but this time she felt sluggish and distracted. However, it was all worth the effort when they were able to lock the database ahead of schedule on June 1. Erin felt like the best part of the whole process was when the study results were revealed internally at Kaso, and she found out that the study was a success! The drug did work to cure pancreatic cancer.

Erin woke up to the smell of smoke and looked over at the alarm clock. It was her first weekend off since the database-lock preparation began, and it was now a quarter to ten on Sunday morning. The sun was beaming through the sides of the blinds in her bedroom, and Dante was missing from the bed. Sandra was at her mom's house for the weekend, so Erin realized that the burning smell must be something that Dante was trying to cook.

Erin sighed and felt exhausted. Although she had gone to bed at ten o'clock, she had woken up three times to use the bathroom. The last time she had gotten up at half past four, and it had taken her nearly two hours to finally fall back to sleep. Erin thought it was ironic that people kept telling her to get as much sleep as possible before the baby was born. She had gradually learned that between having to sleep on her side and the constant pressure on her bladder, she could only sleep for an hour or two at a time.

Erin used the bathroom and brushed her teeth before making her way downstairs. She smiled, greeted Dante with a kiss, and told him good morning.

Dante looked mischievous as he replied, "I know you have worked superhard with your database lock, and I wanted to make you a nice breakfast, but the waffle maker decided that was not going to happen. It burned all my waffle attempts."

Erin looked at the stack of broken, burned waffles on the counter and smiled as she said, "Thank you for trying."

"How about we get dressed and go for brunch at Maple Bistro?" Dante asked.

"Sounds like a great idea," Erin replied.

After getting dressed and ready, Erin and Dante arrived at Maple Bistro an hour later. As they followed the hostess to the back dining area, they were greeted by a loud, "*Surprise!*" Erin was shocked to see her family and friends standing and clapping.

"You burned the waffles on purpose, right?" a teary Erin asked as she hugged Dante.

Dante proudly smiled and nodded yes.

Erin took a long look around the room and saw her parents, her siblings, some longtime friends, and all her friends from work. She was greeted, in quick succession, with hugs from her family: Helen and Owen were first in line, and David, Kelly, Lisa, and Bob followed them. Maggie and Sandra came over at the same time, both looking delighted that Erin had been completely surprised by the baby shower. Lisa had put the two of them in charge of the shower games, and they began preparing ribbons that would be used in a game where guests tried to guess how big Erin's stomach had grown.

As Erin returned to Dante's side, Ronan walked up to Dante and gave him a friendly slap on the back. "You did it! It looks like Erin was completed surprised," he said. "You took the burned-breakfast excuse. Now I have to come up with something so I can pull off a surprise for Kerry's shower!"

Dante laughed and proudly nodded agreement. As Kerry was walking over to join them, Dante quietly said, "Erin, I may need your help with that." They were all chuckling when Kerry joined the circle, and they quickly changed the subject.

Erin left the happily chatting group and walked over to where Molly and Debra were waiting to say hello. She knew they must have been talking about something bad because Debra cringed as a signal to Molly to stop talking as Erin approached.

Molly had said, "I feel so bad for her..." before she noticed Debra's signal and turned around to face Erin. Erin was getting used to people holding back information from her in an effort to avoid upsetting her during her pregnancy. Although it was thoughtful, it was annoying because it almost felt like she were being treated like a child.

Erin smiled and said, "OK, I know you're trying to protect me, but I'm OK. Molly, who are you talking about?"

Molly looked quickly at Debra before saying anything. Finally, she said, "We didn't want to upset you, but we just heard really sad news about Sarah. Things have been so busy lately with the database lock that I had not noticed that Sarah has not been in the office. Apparently, she found out a few months ago that she had pancreatic cancer. She went to senior management after she was diagnosed and asked if she could get some of the study drug from our study. They had to turn her down because it's against federal regulations. She ran out of the building when they turned her down, and she has not returned since."

Erin cringed and said, "I saw her running out of the building that day. I feel so bad that I didn't check on her."

They all agreed to visit Sarah together one day the next week.

Erin spent the next three hours playing silly baby shower games, eating, and unwrapping presents. She had been completely distracted with work recently and hadn't even suspected that Dante was planning the shower with her sister, Lisa. Erin was relieved that Lisa had created her baby registry for her. Erin had no idea what items she needed for a newborn, but she was overwhelmed with gratitude as she unwrapped an unending supply of baby essentials.

As Erin was falling asleep that night, she replayed the entire day in her mind. She could not imagine a better baby shower than the one she had been given. She rested her left hand on her stomach and fell into a deep, dreamless sleep, thinking about how blessed she was to have wonderful family and friends.

30

E rin woke up rested and feeling well on Monday morning. She went through her normal morning routine and was surprised that one of the first e-mails she saw when she sat at her desk was from Sienna. She realized that she hadn't spoken with Sienna in ages. When she opened the e-mail, she saw the message:

Date Sent: June 7, 2004 6:30 a.m.
From: S.Goodman@dmail.com
Subject: Hello

Dear Erin,
Please accept my apology for not summoning you sooner. I would like to meet with you briefly tonight. I will summon you tonight and ex-plain everything in person.
—Sienna

Sandra was staying at her mother's house for the week, and Dante was on call for the night, so Erin had the house to herself. Erin was both excited and nervous about seeing Sienna again. It had been so long that Erin felt out of practice when she closed her eyes that night and began to imagine an outfit to wear. She laughed to herself when she realized she would have to imagine a maternity dress for the warmer climate of Dominica. Erin fell asleep trying to remember everything she wanted to tell Sienna about the changes in her life.

She fell asleep quickly and dreamed she was walking down a flight of industrial metal stairs in a dark hallway. She felt herself slip and landed softly in the field outside of Sienna's home. She immediately noticed some big changes had taken place. At least ten guards were standing in front of the beautiful white staircase. The guards were an assortment of large men of different racial and ethnic backgrounds dressed in identical green fatigues and heavily laden with large machine guns strapped over their shoulders.

As Erin moved closer, she noticed several men in various sniper positions behind trees and rocks in the woods, and they all had their guns trained on her. Erin became nervous and raised her hands in the air in the universal sign of surrender.

The lead guard at the bottom of the staircase smiled and said, "Erin, we were expecting you. You can put your arms down. Sorry for any trouble this extra security may have caused. You are welcome to go up and see Sienna." Erin nodded and carefully slid past the security guards and up the white staircase.

Sienna, who was wearing green cargo pants and a black T-shirt, was waiting for Erin at the top of the staircase. As they walked over to the garden, Erin couldn't believe the difference she saw in Sienna. Her face was drawn, she had large black circles under her eyes, and she looked like she must have lost at least fifteen pounds. However, Sienna smiled widely and looked like a proud parent as she gazed at Erin and her growing pregnancy bump. They greeted each other with a hug, and Sienna gently touched Erin's bump and asked, "How are you feeling?"

Erin replied, "I'm great, but I'm worried about you. What's going on? Are you OK?"

Sienna sighed as they both sat down in the garden. "Things have been incredibly crazy. It feels like everything that can go wrong has gone wrong recently. Last month, the Tara League hacked into our new database. It was a double attack because they deleted large portions of our current Terrent-location information, and our own safety has been compromised because they accessed our DT and Garan contact information." Sienna lowered her head slightly and looked deflated.

Erin felt awful about the news, and her expression must have shown it because Sienna took one look at Erin's face and said, "I shouldn't have told you all this in your condition. I am so sorry!"

Erin tried to regain her composure and quickly added, "No, I'm OK. I just feel so useless. I wish I could do something to help."

Sienna gulped and said, "Unfortunately, your contact information was in the database, and your own security may have been compromised. Please be as careful as possible at all times until we find out who is responsible for this."

Erin replied, "Try not to worry about me. I am always very careful, and our house has a good security alarm, so I should be fine."

Sienna looked a little relieved and said, "The DTC is contacting all the DTs to ask them to be on alert and to be careful. Almost all dream-travel activities have been put on hold for now, too. I am probably going to be very busy over the next few weeks trying to sort things out, so I don't want you to worry or think that we have forgotten about you. We hope that by the time you have the baby, we will be able to re-establish our secure DT network. Then we will get you back on track to becoming a regular dream traveler with regular assignments."

Erin nodded and smiled as convincingly as possible to try to cheer up Sienna.

Sienna looked a little hesitant before continuing, but she added, "Unfortunately, we have some very sad news in our DT family as well. Agnes passed away a few days ago."

"Oh no. What happened?"

Sienna took a deep breath and said, "She had a massive aneurism and died in her sleep. The autopsy showed that the vessel that broke was in an inoperable area of her brain, so there would have been nothing that could have been done to prevent her death."

Erin was in shock and paused before saying, "That is just so sad."

Sienna nodded in agreement and added, "It must have been a horrible weight for Quinn to carry."

Suddenly, several things made sense to Erin in a new way. The reason that the DTC did not allow Agnes to go back and alter time to save her husband from being killed was because her own death was imminent. During the DTC investigation, Quinn must have been the Garan to make the discovery and had to issue the denial of Agnes's request to alter time and save her husband.

Erin replied, "Yes. That is a horrible burden to carry."

"I'm sorry I have to cut this visit short," Sienna continued. "And I'm even more sorry that your security may have been comprised. However, I have to get back to the DTC to try and figure out this breach."

Erin quickly replied, "Sienna, I know that I am limited by my pregnancy, but please let me know if there is anything I can do to help, seriously."

They both stood and hugged good-bye. Sienna looked at Erin with guilty eyes and a worried expression. "Thank you, Erin. Please take care of yourself and the baby."

"I will," Erin confirmed as she lay back on the lounge chair and closed her eyes. When Erin opened her eyes, she was next to Dante in bed. But sleep was hard to come by, and she spent the rest of the night processing all the news she had just heard.

31

Dante yawned as he walked into the bathroom, rubbed his eyes, and said good morning. Erin couldn't stop thinking about the DTC database being compromised but managed a delayed, "Good morning."

Dante was still not fully awake, but he sensed something was amiss with his wife. "What's wrong?"

Erin hesitated before saying, "Sienna summoned me to Dominica last night and let me know that the DTC database has been compromised. She warned me to be careful because there is a chance that someone accessed my contact information."

Dante hesitated for a second and looked like he was going to say something, but instead he turned and walked back out of the bathroom.

Erin glanced at the time on her phone and realized she didn't have time to worry about Dante's reaction. She quickly finished putting on her makeup, grabbed a pair of earrings on her way out of the bedroom, and kissed Dante good-bye. She grabbed her purse, her lunch from the refrigerator, and her car keys, and went out the front door. Erin lowered herself carefully into her car and took a deep breath. At this point in her pregnancy, even simple activities like leaving the house and getting into her car made her breathless. She took another deep breath, started the car, and proceeded to reverse out of the driveway.

Less than two minutes into her drive to work, Erin cursed as she realized that she had left her cell phone on the bathroom counter. She made an illegal U-turn, drove back to the house, and left the car running in the driveway. Erin was resigned to the fact that she was going to be late, and she didn't see any reason to rush and make herself out of breath. She took her time entering the house, walking back up the stairs, and picking up her phone. While she was in the bathroom, Erin heard Dante speaking on his phone in another room. She began moving toward his voice to say good-bye one more time when she heard him say, "Of course I didn't tell Erin. If she gets upset right now, she could go into premature labor."

Erin immediately felt her stomach turn sour as fear spread through her body. Frantic thoughts began to run through her head: "What could be so bad that it would make me go into labor? Is someone sick or hurt? Is everything OK with my family?" Erin tiptoed the last few inches to the doorway of their home office, where she could hear Dante without being seen. The thought that she should probably heed his warning, walk away, and spare herself the trauma of hearing the bad news occurred to her, but she was so curious that she didn't have the willpower to pull away from hearing the rest of Dante's conversation.

"You are right, Olivia. I need to see you today. Can I come over after work this evening? I can tell Erin that I am on call and have to work late."

Erin's fear turned to horror as she processed what Dante was saying to this woman. She felt her body trembling, and a wave of dread coursed through her as her heart burst into a million pieces. Erin covered her mouth and stumbled toward the stairs. She had to get out of the house and to her car without being noticed. She descended the stairs, slipped out the door, and locked it behind herself. Then she got into her car and quietly backed out of the driveway.

Her tears began to pour as soon as the car was moving, and she drove only about sixty seconds before she had to turn off onto a quiet side road. She traveled another two hundred yards until she could no longer see the main road or any homes. Then she pulled her car over to the side of the road. Once she was parked, she let herself sob. How could he do this to her? Why? Erin felt like she was in a pit of horror because of the knowledge that Dante was cheating on her. Her emotions all churned at the same time: pain, embarrassment, betrayal, and rage.

Erin tried to think. She didn't know anyone named Olivia, but obviously Dante was sleeping with this woman. He was planning a secret rendezvous and lying to cover his tracks. Erin felt like an idiot for not picking up on the deception sooner. How many nights had he done this before and said he was on call, when he was really in this woman's arms? How long had this been going on?

Dante had been a little distant lately, but Erin had ignored it because she thought that he was just nervous about the upcoming birth of their child. Erin wondered how she could have been so stupid. How could this happen to her again? Erin thought she had felt the worst pain in her life when she found out that her first husband was cheating on her, but Dante's betrayal was even worse.

Erin alternated between sobbing and trying to catch her breath for an hour before she could pull herself together enough to call work and let them know she would not being coming in today. As she dialed Ronan's office, she quietly prayed that he would not answer his phone so that she could leave a message on his voice mail. However, Ronan picked up on the second ring.

"Hi, Ronan. It's Erin. I'm not feeling that well today, and I am not going to be able to make it into the office." Erin knew that the crying had made her nose stuffy and her throat scratchy, so she definitely sounded believable.

However, Ronan must have detected something else in her voice because he said, "No problem, Erin. Are you OK?"

Erin had a lump in her throat, but she managed to keep her voice steady and replied, "Yes, I just need some time to rest."

Ronan hesitated and soothingly said, "OK, don't worry about anything at work, and get some rest." Erin thanked Ronan, said goodbye, and hung up the phone as quickly as she could. As soon as she hit End on her phone, the next wave of sobbing began.

A minute later, Erin hiccupped and tried to catch her breath as her cell phone began to ring. When she looked at the screen, she saw that Kerry was calling her. Ronan must have known something was wrong and called Kerry. Erin considered not answering the phone, but she also felt like she was going to burst and needed to tell someone what was going on.

Erin cleared her throat and tried to sound calm when she answered the phone. Kerry quickly asked, "Erin, are you really OK?"

The empathy in Kerry's voice was too much for Erin to bear, and she started to cry. Erin couldn't even explain herself between her sobs. Kerry gently asked, "Can I meet you at your house in ten minutes?"

Erin knew that Dante would have left for work by this time. She hiccupped as she agreed. Kerry calmly replied, "Erin, I am going to hang up and get in the car and come over. Try to just relax, and I will be right there."

"OK," Erin mumbled and hung up her cell phone. She took a deep breath and focused on the road as she drove home and parked in the driveway.

Erin stepped into the house and closed the door behind her, but she had only taken a few steps into the foyer when she stopped. A photo of Dante holding her on their honeymoon was hanging on the dining room wall, and the sight of it made her choke up with fresh sobs. Erin grabbed a tissue box from the kitchen counter and sat down at the kitchen table to cry. Within minutes she heard Kerry knock once and open the front door as she said, "Erin, I'm here."

Kerry made her way to the kitchen and put her arms around Erin in a brisk motion. It only took a few minutes for Erin to explain what had happened while Kerry tried her best to soothe Erin.

"I know this is painful, Erin, but you have to think of the baby," Kerry said as she squeezed out a cold cloth in the kitchen sink, brought it over, and placed it on Erin's forehead. Kerry continued, "I've already spoken with Ronan on the way over here, and we were afraid this had happened. We both think our house is the best place for you. Your baby's safety and well-being has to be the highest priority at this point."

Erin felt like she was in a haze and just nodded in response. She went upstairs to pack and heard Kerry downstairs on the phone, whispering to Ronan. Erin was carrying several pairs of slacks to her suitcase when Kerry walked into her bedroom. Kerry took the slacks from Erin's hands and said, "Ronan already said that you're not going back to work. He said that you can start your maternity leave or that, if you insist, you can work from our home, but you need to rest and not worry about work at this point." Erin felt grateful for the respite.

Erin left her car at home, let Kerry drive her back to the McKennas' house, and went through the motions of moving into Kerry and Ronan's home. She felt detached and was grateful when Kerry took charge and guided Erin through the task. Kerry and Ronan had their private nurse midwife, Geraldine, come to the house to check Erin and make sure everything was OK with the baby.

When the nurse said that Erin was having mild, sporadic contractions, Kerry's face hardened with a determined look. Erin was put on bed rest and given a mild sedative. Erin agreed with Kerry's suggestion that she give her cell phone to Kerry to screen her calls.

Erin was drifting in and out of a dream when she overheard someone speaking. She began to awaken and realized she was sleeping in Kerry's guest room. The guest room was large and beautifully decorated with a desk and chair on one side of the room and a small sitting area on the other side. She could hear Kerry's muffled voice on the phone as she drifted into and out of a light sleep.

She heard Kerry raise her voice and say, "You should be ashamed of yourself, Dante! Save your lies and excuses for your lawyer. Your selfish behavior is disgusting, especially when your wife is pregnant with your child!" The reality of Erin's situation washed over her again like a harsh acid rain, and she sobbed quietly into her pillow until the sedative pulled her back into sleep.

32

Molly closed her eyes and took a deep breath. She had taken a stress-management course a few months prior, and she began the exercise she had learned to use to help her deal with stress. She closed her eyes and breathed slowly and deeply as she imagined a peaceful, warm tropical beach. Molly tried to imagine what the waves would sound like as they gently lapped the beautiful, white-sand beach.

The imagery lasted about thirty seconds before the worries filled her head: How was she going to be able to finish all the work that needed to be done to meet the study time lines without Erin? How would she find time to train the new consultant who was hired to help while Erin was on maternity leave? Was Erin going to be OK?

Her stress level shot up again at the last question. She mentally replayed the phone call she had received from her sister earlier in the day. Kerry had explained that Erin had caught Dante having an affair with some woman named Olivia and that Erin was staying at Kerry's house to try to remain as calm and healthy as possible for the rest of her pregnancy.

Although Kerry had explained it all to Molly, it just didn't make sense. She had seen Dante and Erin together many times, and they made such a wonderful couple. Molly felt unsettled because if Dante could cheat on Erin, what would keep Jack from cheating on her in the future?

Molly looked at her watch and saw that it was half past three. Knowing she had lost focus, she packed up her laptop and vowed to go home and finish reviewing study data after she ate dinner and took a shower. Molly grabbed her bags and began walking out of the building. However, she couldn't help feeling remorseful as she passed Erin's empty cubical. Molly decided that a quick stop at her sister's house on the way home would make her feel better.

Previously, she had been feeling just a little jealous that Erin and Kerry had grown so close in the past few months, but knowing they had their pregnancies in common, she had accepted that both Kerry and Erin had a lot to share at the moment. Molly hoped that after the baby was born and Erin returned to work, things would go back to normal, and they would get to spend more time together again.

As Molly walked to the parking lot, she saw Dante pacing by her car. She was shocked by his haggard appearance. Dante was wearing a dark-gray suit, but the tie was loosened at the neck and skewed to the side. His eyes looked both swollen and crazed as he began walking in her direction. Anger welled up in Molly at the man who had hurt her friend at a time in life when they should be happy and celebrating the upcoming birth of their child. Kerry had warned Molly that Dante was upset and wanted to see Erin and that she had warned him to stay away from their house. Molly discreetly patted her pants pocket where she had put her phone, knowing that she could quickly call 9-1-1 if she needed to.

As Dante grew nearer, Molly saw something puzzling. She realized Dante's eyes were swollen from crying and that he looked scared. She had expected arrogance or denial, but she saw the face of a man who looked like he was terrified by what was happening to him.

He held his hands up in almost a surrendering position as he neared her and quickly said, "Molly, please give me a second to explain."

Molly wanted to remain hard as steel and ignore him as she pushed on toward her car, but part of her melted at his obvious distress, and she asked, "Dante, how could you do this to Erin?"

"That's the thing. I swear I didn't do anything," Dante replied. "Please give me five minutes to explain." Acting against Kerry's warning, Molly hesitated and stopped. She felt she should probably say no to Dante, but she couldn't ignore the helpless, pleading look in his eyes.

Dante took her hesitation as agreement and said, "I think I know what Erin overheard today, and the conversation was not what she thought. I think Erin is experiencing some type of gestational psychosis."

Molly could feel her blood boiling as she realized she had made a mistake by letting Dante explain. He had chosen the typical cheating-spouse excuse that he was innocent and Erin was crazy or paranoid and had imagined the whole thing. Molly realized she should have listened to her sister and felt like an idiot for stopping to hear what he had to say. Molly huffed out, "You are a real asshole!" She stomped past Dante and walked to her car.

Dante panicked at Molly's reaction and belted out, "Erin thinks she is time traveling when she sleeps!"

Molly froze in her tracks. Thinking she may have misheard him, her pace slowed.

Dante saw Molly hesitate and continued, "I am serious. She thinks that she's a dream traveler and that she can travel through time while she sleeps! All of this nonsense started when she found out she was pregnant, and it has continued through the course of her pregnancy. I was hoping it would stop, but after a while I consulted a psychiatrist."

Molly looked around the parking lot and saw a few people in the distance, and she didn't want them to hear Dante shouting about Erin's business. "OK," Molly said in a resigned voice. "I'll listen to your story, but come sit in my car."

With a beep, Molly opened the doors to her black Volvo S40 and sat in the driver's seat. Dante quickly sat in the passenger's seat. Molly took a deep breath and said, "I'm confused. What happened to Erin during her pregnancy?"

Dante composed himself and attempted to explain. "When she first found out she was pregnant, she claimed that she was a dream traveler and that she could travel through time when she was sleeping. I didn't know what to do with that information, so I chalked it up to hormones and her excitement and just ignored it. Then it got worse, and she was waking up from dreams with stories of where she had traveled and said that people called Garans were summoning her in her dreams.

"She was completely convinced that these dream-traveling experiences were real! She was hallucinating, and I began to get worried that she would hurt herself or the baby during the hallucinations. So I reached out to the head of the psychiatry unit in the hospital, Olivia Rossi, and explained everything to her. Dr. Rossi confirmed that it sounded like gestational psychosis and that confronting Erin while she was pregnant would cause her psychological trauma and potentially cause her to go into labor."

Dante's shoulders slumped as he almost whispered, "Looking back, that would have been better than the psychological trauma that she must be experiencing right now. Dr. Rossi recommended that I call her immediately after each hallucination to ensure that they did not progress to psychotic behavior that could put Erin or the baby in danger. Erin overheard me today trying to schedule a visit with Dr. Rossi because Erin just had another episode this morning and thought she had been summoned to a tropical island last night.

"I have had to lie to Erin and say I'm working late to fit in these appointments, so what she overheard this morning must have sounded incriminating. I received a voice mail from Kerry saying that Erin overheard me talking to my mistress and that she had moved into Ronan and Kerry's house. Kerry said that, for the good of Erin's health, she was holding her cell phone and filtering her calls.

"I tried to explain the whole mess to Kerry, but she wouldn't let me. She said that if I try to come to their house, she is going to call the police! If I could talk to Erin, I could explain everything! I could even introduce her to Olivia Rossi…this whole thing is completely out of control, and Erin is suffering for no reason. Please, Molly, you have to help me!"

Molly nodded, but she remained silent. She had not said a word and was still processing everything she had heard. Then Molly whispered, "Dante, you don't have to convince me. I believe you."

Dante's expression changed to relief.

"I believe you and what you have said, but you should not tell anyone else what Erin has told you about dream traveling." Molly paused and then took the plunge. "You should not tell anyone else because it's true. I know this because I am part of this other world of people who can travel through time. From what I have heard, the dream travelers have severe punishments when people break their confidentiality, so you really should not tell anyone else what she told you."

Dante's expression had shifted from relief to fear.

Molly continued, "Until just now I had no idea that Erin was a dream traveler because I was born a Terrent, and we are kind of the enemies of the dream travelers. I have tried to do everything I can do to bury that part of my life and to separate myself from that dark world. I hate that I was born a Terrent, and in fact, I'm kind of the black sheep of my family."

"Stop, please," Dante begged as he put his hands up and rubbed his temple. "No, go ahead and tell me. What in the world are you talking about?"

Molly started from the beginning and explained how dream travelers and Terrents existed and how the DTC and the Tara League worked. She explained how anytime a person hears a ringing sound that a dream traveler is in the near proximity and how that ringing sound is irresistable to Terrents. She also explained how she refused to participate in the Tara League (TL) and took daily fluoride supplements to keep her Terrent tendencies dormant. Molly explained that Ronan and Kerry were Terrents, too, but they were her complete opposite. They were working hard to increase their status within the

Tara League. Ronan had actually just been elected as a high council-man and had his sights set on some day becoming president of the Tara League.

Dante still looked confused as he said, "I am not sure I under-stand all of this, but I can't process this right now. I just need to see my wife."

Molly said, "I will get you into Kerry's house." Dante's whole de-meanor changed as he heard the words he had been waiting to hear.

Dante quickly said, "Thank you so much, Molly. I know Erin will understand once I explain this whole situation to her."

Molly continued, "I will go in first and just tell Kerry the truth and that this has been a complete misunderstanding. Kerry and Ronan and all the other pregnant Terrent parents have been very excited lately because there is a famous prophecy that states that the most powerful Garan will be born during the year of the first tetrad of the twenty-first century, and this Garan will be born into the hands of a Terrent. All pregnant Terrent couples are secretly hoping that they are pregnant with this Garan. So I imagine that Ronan and Kerry will be relieved to get this situation cleared up so that they can focus on the birth of their own child.

"This prophecy is exciting to Terrents because if Terrents could raise and control their own Garan, they could control their travel both into the past and into the future. There would be no bounds to what the TL could achieve. I think it's a bad idea, personally, and if my new nephew or niece is this Garan, I will definitely not allow the TL to hurt or use him or her in any way."

Dante shook his head slightly from side to side. "I don't think I can handle any more news or prophecies at this point. I just want to bring Erin home and put this whole thing behind us."

"I understand. Do you want to follow me in your car to their house? It would probably be easiest if you stay outside while I talk to my sister, but I can call your cell phone as soon as I bring Kerry up to speed." Dante agreed, and they exchanged cell phone numbers as they parted.

33

M olly could not believe the day's turn of events. She was slowly driving to Kerry's house, and her thoughts were all centered on Erin. It was so strange that Erin was a dream traveler. According to what Dante had described, Erin must have found out just recently. Molly felt sorry for Erin. It would be difficult to keep all this new information to herself, and the one person she was allowed to tell, Dante, hadn't believed her. Molly felt incredibly relieved that Dante had not cheated on Erin. She pulled into Ronan and Kerry's driveway and saw Dante in her rearview mirror, parking his car on the street.

Molly got out of her car, walked to the front door, and rang the bell. Within seconds Kerry answered the door, with her cell phone pressed to her ear, saying, "Yes, I agree, but we need to discuss the meeting agenda and summarize the regional updates in a high-level format."

Molly guessed that Kerry was on a TL call with someone. Kerry silently air-kissed her sister's cheek, pointed to the guest room, and leaned her head to the side and shut her eyes to mime Erin sleeping. Kerry silently mouthed, "Do you want something to drink?"

Molly nodded and pointed to the basement door, knowing her sister kept a large supply of ginger ale in the refrigerator in the basement. Kerry nodded and waddled slowly back to the kitchen as Molly opened the door to the basement.

Molly thought about how her family was always hoping that she would embrace her Terrent talents and start participating in the TL. They always tried to keep her abreast of the current gossip and activities. They had told her that the TL had made a major breakthrough recently when they hacked into the DTC database.

Molly went down the flight of stairs, noticing the familiar, mild chemical smell, and hit the light switch. The basement was unfinished, and Kerry and Ronan mostly used it for storage. She looked at the floor-to-ceiling gray metal shelves that lined the two sidewalls of the room. They were meticulously stacked with canned goods, cleaning fluids, and kitchen products, all ordered by size with the labels facing forward. A faint smell of gasoline drifted in from the door on her right that led to the garage. The door to the boiler room was straight ahead, and the refrigerator was to the left of that door. As Molly pulled open the refrigerator door and grabbed a can of ginger ale from the top shelf, she wondered if Ronan, as a high council member, was aware that Erin was a DT.

Molly's stomach felt upset after all the craziness of the day, and she hoped that the ginger ale would help her feel better. As Molly opened the can, her charm bracelet caught on the can's opener tab. The bracelet fell from her wrist, and the gold chain hit the floor. Molly cursed as the heart charm that Jack had given her skidded under the door into the boiler room. The bracelet was the first gift Jack had given her, so Molly quickly formulated a plan to take the bracelet to the jewelry store tomorrow to have it repaired before Jack noticed it was missing. She just needed to recover the heart charm.

There had been a spider infestation in the boiler room when Ronan and Kerry bought their house years ago, and Molly—who was deathly afraid of spiders—had sworn she would never go into that room. She took a deep breath and cringed as she opened the door and walked into the boiler room to retrieve the charm.

When she pulled the string to turn on the lightbulb, she was pleasantly surprised to see that the room was clean and free of spiders. Molly didn't see the charm on the floor and guessed it must have slid between the several large cardboard boxes on the floor. Molly whispered as she read the side of the box, "Hollywood Studio Productions?" Molly wondered if the TL was putting on a play. She smiled as she saw her heart charm behind one of the boxes and quickly picked it up. As she was about to leave the room, her curiosity got the best of her when she noticed the box lids were not sealed closed, and she gently lifted one of the cardboard flaps.

Molly lifted out some beige-colored cloth and saw that she was holding some sort of a woman's girdle with a soft, round bump attached to the section that would cover the belly. The round bump felt and looked just like real skin. Confusion and dread filled Molly's mind as she opened the flaps of the other boxes and realized that she was looking at a full collection of progressively bigger pregnancy prostheses. Molly jumped when her cell phone rang, and she saw that it was Dante calling.

"Can I come in?" Dante asked as soon as Molly opened her phone.

"I don't know...not yet," Molly mumbled as she stared at the boxes in front of her.

"Molly? What is wrong?"

34

rin woke up to a tightening across her stomach followed by a sharp cramping. She knew she was having contractions, but it was too early for her to have the baby. The gravity of her situation threatened to wash over her again, and she realized that she had to protect her baby from her emotions. She immediately started putting walls up in her mind to compartmentalize her stress, and she tried to focus on what she thought her baby would look like. She longed to meet the love of her life that was growing inside her, and she felt a gentle movement as the baby shifted positions, as if the baby were responding to her thoughts.

Erin went to the bathroom and washed her face. Every time her mind wanted to stray to thoughts of her marriage, she used all her energy to focus on trying to picture the baby. She brushed her hair, straightened her clothes, and walked out of the guest room. As Erin turned into the kitchen, she saw Kerry talking on the phone. Kerry quickly said, "I have to call you back." And she hung up the phone.

Kerry greeted her with a look of concern and asked, "How are you feeling? Did you have any more contractions?"

Erin replied, "I just woke up to one, but none followed that one. I have decided that I need to focus on the baby at this point, and I am going to try to keep myself from thinking about anything else." Erin paused and added, "I just want to thank you again for taking me in and for taking care of me. I hope I haven't caused you any distress."

Kerry stretched out her arms to Erin and gave her a half hug over their swollen bellies. "Please don't waste another minute worrying about me. I'm fine, and I actually like having you here. I feel so much better now that you're under Geraldine's care." Kerry nodded in the direction of an older Asian woman, dressed in white scrubs and a lab coat, who was typing on a laptop at the kitchen table. "Geraldine is amazing, and she really is the best option for ensuring you have a wonderful birthing experience."

Geraldine accepted the compliment with a proud nod and returned her attention to her laptop on the table.

Erin saw Molly coming through the door with a can of soda in her hand. Erin's eyes welled up a little as Molly greeted her with a gentle hug. Within a fraction of a second, Kerry chirped, "Molly, Erin just had another set of contractions, so please don't talk about anything that will upset her."

Molly had a strained expression on her face as she uttered, "I understand." She focused on Erin and asked, "Erin, can I talk to you alone for a minute about a work thing? Nothing stressful, just something I need to talk to you about."

"Oh, sure," Erin agreed as they walked in the direction of the guest room where Erin was staying. Kerry eyed Molly suspiciously as they moved down the hallway and entered the room.

As Erin sat on the bed, Molly closed the door behind her and sat in a chair by the bed. Molly's strained expression transitioned into one of great sadness. She stared into Erin's eyes and asked sincerely, "Is everything OK with the baby?"

Erin's hand went to her stomach, and she gently rubbed her belly as she responded, "Yes. I'm having sporadic contractions right now, but as long as they don't become regular and my water doesn't break, the baby is OK."

Molly nodded and began, "I am going to explain something to you as quickly and easily as possible." She took a deep breath and said, "Erin, Dante didn't cheat on you. You have been telling him some unusual stuff lately, and he thought you were experiencing gestational psychosis. He began talking secretly to a female psychiatrist, Dr. Olivia Rossi. That is who you heard him talking to earlier today. And by the way, Dr. Rossi has been happily married for fifty years and is in her late seventies, so she is not exactly a temptress."

Erin took a deep breath, and her whole demeanor brightened. "I feel like such an idiot! Oh gosh, I have to talk to Dante!" Erin began reaching for her purse and realized that Kerry had her cell phone and was screening her calls.

"Can I use your cell phone? I can't believe I did this to Dante!"

Molly handed her phone to Erin. As Erin dialed, her forehead puckered in confusion. "That doesn't make sense. Why didn't Dante explain that to Kerry earlier today when he called?"

Molly's face hardened as she quietly spoke, "Erin, when you get off the phone, I have to share something with you…and I'm just hoping it doesn't upset you…"

Erin began crying as she spoke, "Dante, I am so sorry…"

Kerry entered the room without knocking, carrying a tray of teacups and cookies. "I have chamomile tea for everyone." Kerry stiffened as she saw Erin, tears running down her face and speaking into Molly's phone. She quickly shouted for Ronan and turned her piercing gaze to Molly. "What did you say to her?"

Kerry set down the tea tray, hurried to Erin, and firmly took the cell phone. "Erin, please lie back down. You must rest."

Ronan was in the doorframe by now, and he added, "Yes, Erin, please relax and lie down. We have to do what is best for the baby." He moved into the room as Erin slowly slid farther back on the bed.

Erin looked up at Kerry and Ronan with a weak smile and said, "I can't thank you both enough for your kindness and generosity, but I just found out that I made a huge mistake. Dante has not been cheating on me. I'm so sorry for putting everyone through this ordeal, but I need to see my husband right away."

Kerry glared at Molly as she moved in her direction. A salesman's smile spread across Ronan's face as he said, "I think we may be moving too fast here. I wouldn't believe anything that Molly has told you. We all know that she can be a bit of an airhead from time to time. The best thing is for you to get some rest. Lie back down and take a nap, and we will call Dante and ask him to come pick you up."

Molly countered, "Oh, no need, Ronan. Dante is waiting outside right now."

The fake smile dropped from Ronan's face, and his expression grew stern. "Molly, do you really want to upset Erin like this? I know for a fact that her husband has been cheating on her, and of course he's going to lie about it."

"*Step away from my wife right now!*" boomed a voice from the doorway, where Dante stood with a crimson face, his hands clenched in fists at his sides.

Ronan's face was strained. He spun on his heel and shouted, "*This is my house and...*" He never finished his sentence because Dante sprinted forward and punched him. There was an audible crack as Dante's fist made contact with Ronan's chin. Ronan's head reeled back from the impact, but he quickly retaliated by tackling Dante and pummeling him.

As the two men locked into a brawl, Kerry dived at Molly, wrapped her hands around her neck, and screeched, "Why did you let him in? You have always been a failure, and now you are dead to me!"

Molly choked and barely was able to whisper, "How could you do this?" She desperately reached around Kerry's waist, felt the plastic seam, and pulled at it. The prosthetic baby bump slid to the side as Kerry gasped and reached for her stomach. Molly made a wheezing sound as she took a deep breath. Kerry's eyes blazed as she realized her secret was out. She tackled Molly and attacked her with renewed strength. Kerry looked like an animal, repeatedly banging Molly's head against the floor and continuing to choke her.

Erin was frozen in a state of shock for a moment, but she soon looked around the room for something to use as a weapon. She was picking up the chair that was in front of the desk when she heard a sickening crack as Ronan broke Dante's nose. Dante's body went limp, and Ronan continued to punch his head.

Frantic, Erin lifted the chair above her head, but Geraldine darted in front of her and jammed a syringe into Ronan's neck. Ronan grabbed Geraldine's wrist, but it was too late. Whatever she had injected Ronan with caused him to immediately lose strength. His eyes closed, and he collapsed on the floor next to Dante.

Erin dropped the chair as pain gripped her middle. She held her stomach, crying and moaning, and stared at the puddle of water on the floor. Her water had just broke. When she looked up, she saw that Geraldine was already behind Kerry. But when Geraldine reached into her pocket for a second syringe, Kerry sensed the danger and released Molly. She grabbed Geraldine's arm and began to twist it behind her back. Molly rolled on her side, desperately gasping for air. Erin could hear her wheeze with each labored breath.

Kerry's strength and brutality were shocking. There was a sickening sound of bone cracking as she broke Geraldine's wrist, and Geraldine let out a primal scream of pain. Kerry shrieked, "How *dare* you! I should have known you were a double agent because your whole family is nothing but white-trash Terrents..."

Suddenly, Kerry's eyes rolled back in her head, and she released her hands from Geraldine's arm and collapsed to the floor. Geraldine had managed to use her other arm to inject Kerry. She threw the syringe down on Kerry's unconscious body and tenderly cradled her broken wrist.

35

Molly had an arm around Erin and was trying to support her weight as much as possible and run at the same time. As they exited the house, Molly hoarsely whispered, "My car is right here." Molly helped Erin into the backseat, quickly got in the driver's seat, and started the car. A second later she was reversing down the driveway as quickly as she could.

"Dante will be all right, Erin, I'm sure of it," soothed Molly. "Geraldine said that Dante has a broken nose, and the pain caused him to pass out. Other than that he checked out fine. She feels useless for not being able to deliver the baby, but with her broken wrist, she isn't in the best condition to help. She said that we had plenty of time to get you to the hospital, though.

"Geraldine is going to call the DTC special team to clean up this whole mess. Once they take over, Dante and Geraldine will meet us at the hospital. However, since your contractions are two minutes apart, we need to get you to the hospital now."

As they cruised down the road, Molly glanced at Erin in the rearview mirror and softly said, "Dante told me that you're a dream traveler, and I know what that means because I am a Terrent."

Erin's expression turned to fear, and she glanced at the door handle and lock while continuing to pant through her contraction. Molly noticed Erin's glance and explained, "Don't worry, Erin. I have never agreed with the Terrent lifestyle, and I have intentionally medicated with fluoride to mask my Terrent abilities. However, Kerry and Ronan are very active and powerful Terrents."

Erin relaxed as her contraction passed, and she was mentally digesting what Molly had just said.

Suddenly, she moaned in pain and gasped, "I think things are moving faster than they are supposed to! I'm feeling pressure, and I think that only happens when the baby is crowning! Please, help me!"

Molly knew they were at least ten minutes from the hospital, so she pulled the car to the side of the road and called 9-1-1. Molly had a vague idea from movies that the person delivering the baby usually had boiling water and towels. Molly only had an old sweatshirt and a half-empty bottle of water. She had no idea what she was supposed to do with them. The emergency operator offered to stay on the phone and assist her, but it was hard for Molly to focus on what she was saying.

Molly put her cell phone on speaker and followed the operator's instructions. She knew the baby was coming, but she was still amazed to see a small head appear. The head was quickly followed by shoulders, and the next thing Molly knew, she was holding a baby in her arms. Molly had tears running down her face as she wrapped the baby in her sweatshirt. He was a perfect baby boy. His face turned red as he began to wail in protest at his new surroundings. Molly gingerly placed the wrapped baby in Erin's arms as the ambulance pulled alongside the car.

As the EMT workers attended to mother and baby, another ambulance pulled over to the side of the road, and Geraldine and Dante jumped out—against the wishes of the EMTs who were assisting them. Dante had a bandage on his nose and swollen circles under his eyes, but he limped quickly to his wife. A huge smile broke across his face, and tears welled up in his eyes when the EMT placed his freshly cleaned and blanket-swaddled son in his arms.

Molly signaled to Geraldine, and they moved to a private area on the side of the road. "Is my sister OK? I know she seems insane, but

I swear something was wrong. She is not like that. I think she's been brainwashed by Ronan and has lost touch with reality."

Geraldine replied, "I think she has been following Ronan in some cultlike way because when she woke up and was separated from Ronan, she confessed to everything and appears to be remorseful. Kerry confessed that after the Tara League alerted them that Erin was a new dream traveler, Ronan started hacking Erin's Internet usage at work. When he saw her reviewing maternity information on the company's human-resource website, he illegally accessed Erin's health insurance account and confirmed her pregnancy and the expected date of delivery.

"Kerry said that she recently found out she would never be able to have children of her own and that they were getting ready to tell your family of their plans to try to adopt a baby. That's when Ronan convinced her that Erin's baby would be the perfect baby for them because of the potential for the child to be a DT. Kerry kept her infertility a secret and staged a fake pregnancy with a due date that was similar to Erin's due date.

"Although Kerry had asked me to perform a home delivery for her, she said that her obstetrician was going to take care of her until the date of delivery. So today was the first time I had visited their home, and I only examined Erin today. Obviously, it makes sense now that Kerry didn't want me to examine her."

Molly thought of the boxes of pregnancy prostheses, and she nodded in agreement.

Geraldine continued, "I enter the names of all my patients into an electronic medical-records system, and this system is secretly tied to the DTC database. Today when I entered Kerry and Ronan's address and Erin's name into the system, I received an immediate notification that Erin was a dream traveler. This was followed by instructions from the DTC to remove Erin from the premises as soon as possible. I wasn't sure how I was going to accomplish that task until I heard the shouting from the guest room. I quickly thought of using the IV pain medications I carry to fill several syringes with tranquilizer-sized doses.

"Thank God I was able to use the medication to subdue them because Ronan's plan was pure evil. He wanted me to assist Erin in the birth, and then his plan was to excuse me after Erin's delivery. Ronan and Kerry were going to drug Erin, take her baby, and then set fire to the home. They had cleverly set up the most explosive household items in the garage, which is right below the guest room. The intensity of the explosion would have destroyed all evidence of their crime. They were going to say that they weren't home at the time because they were en route to the hospital when Kerry delivered in the car. Since everyone has seen Kerry pregnant for months, no one would ever discover that the baby was not hers."

Molly shook her head and muttered, "I can't believe this…"

Geraldine nodded and said, "I know. It seems crazy. As a Terrent double agent planted by the Dream Travelers Council years ago, I have been working undercover to identify Terrent births for years, and I've never come across something like this before. I'm just glad we were able to prevent this disaster." Geraldine smiled as she said, "The good news is that the DTC has already framed Ronan for a crime that will keep him in prison for the rest of his life. They have set up false records showing that he illegally transferred two million dollars of Kaso Pharmaceutical funds to a fraudulent vendor company that he owned. As we were leaving, the cops were arriving to arrest him."

Molly sighed in relief and asked, "What about my sister? Can the DTC be lenient on her?"

Geraldine answered, "Since she did provide a full confession, and she was most likely reprogrammed psychologically by Ronan, the DTC has committed her to a facility for psychological counseling and therapy. They will reevaluate her case at the completion of her therapy."

Molly stated, "I know that she just broke your wrist and tried to strangle me, but I'm relieved that the DTC has given her a reprieve. She will be a different person without Ronan in her life; she really is a good person, deep down."

36

Baby Boy Brusca rode in the ambulance with his parents to the hospital. Erin held him in her arms and continued to marvel at the little human they had created. She soaked in every detail of his beautiful, long eyelashes, his tiny lips, and his little button nose. She held his hands and counted his fingers and proceeded to do the same with his toes.

He had been quickly cleaned by the EMTs at the car, but as Erin passed him to Dante, she noticed a smudge on his foot and wiped it with her finger. Erin held his foot closer and gasped when she noticed that it wasn't a smudge, but a triangle-shaped, tan birthmark on the sole of his foot. She lifted the blanket and confirmed with dread that he had a matching triangular-shaped birthmark on the sole of his other foot. Erin shook as she realized that her son was a Garan, and he had been born into the hands of a Terrent.

www.ingramcontent.com/pod-product-compliance
Lightning Source LLC
Chambersburg PA
CBHW070822120626
46556CB00002B/621